STILL GO CRAZY

Swoon Series

J.H. CROIX

J.H. CROIX

 Created with Vellum

I don't often have playlists for my titles, but to put you in the mood of this story, you might want to play I Go Crazy by Paul Davis, 1977.
xoxo

Sign up for my newsletter for information on new releases & get a FREE copy of one of my books!

http://jhcroixauthor.com/subscribe/

Follow me!
jhcroix@jhcroix.com
https://www.bookbub.com/authors/j-h-croix
https://www.facebook.com/jhcroix
https://www.instagram.com/jhcroix/

Chapter One

GRACE

My ancient cat, Wayne, let out a plaintive meow.

"Seriously?" I countered, turning to glare at Wayne.

Wayne cocked his head to the side before lifting his haunches slightly and settling back down. His only reply was another meow. This time, his annoyance was quite clear.

I eyed the tree from where I stood on the back deck. It was a lovely dogwood situated in the backyard. "Wayne, how the hell did you get up there?"

Although I didn't expect an answer, I was genuinely curious. According to the vet, Wayne was close to blind as a result of his cataracts. He was approaching seventeen years old, so it was surprising he could see anything, much less climb a tree.

I rested a hand on my hip, contemplating my options. "I need to get to work, you know," I called over to him.

Wayne didn't even deign that with a response. My father had gotten Wayne for me when I was twelve, and Wayne had come to live with me in this duplex after I graduated from college. My parents bought the duplex when they had a brief separation while I was in college. After they reunited, they kept it and rented it out. When my father passed away, my mother deeded the whole place to me.

I'd arranged for a property management company to rent out the other half of the duplex because I hated trying to screen tenants. I wished I knew who'd moved in the day before because I could've used some help at the moment.

With another long look at Wayne on his perch, I glanced at my watch and contemplated if I had enough time to do this. It didn't really matter if I did because I wasn't leaving until Wayne was safely inside.

Wayne meowed again, and I glared at him from the porch. "You're an idiot, you know?"

This wasn't the first time Wayne had

climbed into his favorite tree and been unable to get down. I had an excellent view from the deck upstairs. The duplex was built into a sloping hill with the living space on the upper floor with a garage that was nothing more than a glorified storage space on the lower floor. Stepping back inside, I jogged down the stairs and snagged the ladder before walking out into the backyard. I leaned the ladder against the tree and commenced the rescue of my adventurous, geriatric cat.

I climbed to the top of the ladder with my feet firmly hooked into the rungs. I was reaching for Wayne when he meowed and shifted just as I leaned over to get him. In a flash, one of my feet wobbled, I lost my balance, and reflexively grabbed for the closest sturdy branch. Unfortunately, I accidentally kicked the ladder loose when my weight shifted.

"Wayne!" I exclaimed as I found myself dangling from the tree branch. Granted, I was only maybe ten feet in the air, but I didn't really want to drop from this height. Wayne walked closer, leaning his head down to nuzzle my hand. He peered at me, his foggy round blue eyes assessing me.

"You know, Wayne, you can't keep doing this," I said conversationally as I assessed my situation. My only actual option was dropping to the ground.

Just as I was considering whether or not I might break an ankle in the process of doing so, I heard a voice.

"Grace?"

I knew that voice. Oh-so-very well.

My pulse took off at a gallop, and my stomach knotted immediately. Of all the times for Boone Reeves to see me, it just had to be now. I promptly decided I'd rather dive straight to the ground and break my ankle than ask for his help. As soon as I made that decision, I looked down and reconsidered. The grass was just far enough away that if I didn't land well, it would be unpleasant.

More unfortunate than me encountering Boone at this particular moment was the fact that Boone was a rescue kind of guy. Peering over my shoulder, I saw him jogging off the back porch of the duplex.

What the hell is he doing here?

Boone stopped at my feet and glanced up. Without even asking, he quickly propped the ladder against the tree and climbed it, reaching for my hand.

"Come on," he said. "I'll get you down."

"Boone, that ladder can't hold both of us."

"Sure it can. Come on, Grace."

Wayne meowed loudly and then started purring. My cat was fucking purring at the sight of my ex. The man who all but threw my love in the trash.

Boone's face cracked with a grin. "Nice to see you again, Wayne." His gaze swung back to me. "Grace, your arms are shaking. Let me help you."

My arms *were* shaking, and my hands were tired. I didn't want help from anybody, most adamantly *not* Boone. But I prided myself on being a smart girl.

Biting back a sigh, I shifted slightly, and Boone wrapped his arm around my waist. The feel of his strong, steady touch was like a live wire, electrifying my entire body.

I had successfully avoided too much contact with Boone for almost a year now. Without a doubt, being this up close and personal with him was a special kind of hell.

"Boone." His name just slipped out, my voice sounding frayed. I was getting anxious as he tugged me a little closer.

"Grace, I've got you. I promise."

The thing was, I believed him. Boone wouldn't drop me. He might've once kicked my love to the curb as though it had never mattered, but he wouldn't let me fall. Truth be told, he wouldn't let anyone in my situation fall. He was strong and resourceful, oozing with that save-any-damsel-in-distress vibe.

I stopped resisting, and Boone pulled me even closer. I finally let go of the tree branch completely, both out of resignation and sheer tiredness. My arms were shaking and a strange tingling sensation was taking over. I made a mental note to start doing pull-ups, almost embarrassed at how poor my upper body strength was.

With one hand on the ladder, Boone held me close as I fumbled to get my feet on the rungs.

"I gotcha," he said.

The raspy vibration of his voice, so close to my ear, sent an inconvenient shiver chasing over my skin. In a matter of seconds, we were on the ground. I stepped back abruptly, my legs almost giving out. I didn't know if my shakiness was from hanging onto the branch ...or from getting too close to Boone.

My cheeks were hot, but I willed myself to look at him. I wasn't going to be a coward. I met his gaze head-on, trying and failing to take a deep breath. My body was in an all-out war with my mind.

Boone was everything I remembered and

more. It wasn't that I hadn't seen him recently. It was more that I hadn't allowed myself more than a passing glance. The young man he'd once been had been honed into much *more* of a man. Tall with a rangy build, his shaggy dark blond hair was rumpled with the ends brushing his shoulders. He moved with an unconscious grace and was all lithe, lean muscle.

Boone looked at me, his dark chocolate gaze coasting over me, warm and concerned. "You okay?" he asked.

I swallowed and nodded. "Yeah. Thanks for that."

He gestured up toward Wayne. "I'm guessing you were trying to get Wayne down."

Butterflies had taken up residence in my belly, an unsettled bunch of them. Wrapping my arms around my waist, I gripped my elbows tightly, trying to find an anchor inside the storm of emotions buzzing through my body.

With Boone's eyes holding mine, the beginning of a grin teasing at the corners of his mouth, I felt as if I had stepped through a window in time—back to our senior year of high school when Boone was my boyfriend. We spent many afternoons together, and

Boone had been endlessly amused by Wayne's antics.

"Yeah," I finally managed to reply, the word coming out ragged.

"I'll get him." Boone turned, climbing the ladder before I could even respond. In another moment, I heard him murmuring to Wayne as my cat nestled into the crook of his arm, staying put as if he were a well-trained, obedient cat.

"Where should I take him?" Boone asked once he was standing on the ground in front of me again. Wayne, the disloyal cat that he was, was purring up a storm now and rubbing his chin against Boone's shoulder.

I had to unstick myself and climb back through that window in time to the present. "Right this way," I said, turning and almost running into the house. Coming to a skidding stop on the back deck, I looked up at Boone. "I can take him."

Wayne, as if he knew what I meant, meowed and burrowed deeper into Boone's arms. When I tried to reach for him, Wayne was having none of it, shifting away from me and burying his face against Boone. Boone chuckled.

With a sigh, I gestured for Boone to follow me inside. "Come on up."

The downstairs of the duplex contained a shared entryway and two separate staircases that led to the upstairs on each side. I had a sickening feeling that the property management company had rented it to Boone.

Opening the door upstairs, I held it as Boone walked through. At that point, Wayne leaped out of his arms and immediately climbed into his small bed on the windowsill.

"Well, thanks again," I said as I turned back to Boone.

This was supposed to be the point where Boone took the hint and left. He didn't.

Cocking his head to the side, his gaze swept over my face. "I'm just now realizing that you're my neighbor," he said softly.

Chapter Two

BOONE

Grace Lakes stood before me, her mesmerizing silver eyes flashing and her chin lifting with a stubborn tilt. My entire body felt like an antenna tuned to one frequency—Grace.

I wanted a reckoning with her, but I hadn't counted on it being like this.

"You rented the other half of the duplex?" she asked, each word enunciated clearly in that soft, crisp tone of hers.

Most people who had a Southern accent had words with round edges, where everything kind of sloughed off slowly, moving like honey. With Grace, she had the twang, but her enunciation was so precise and clear. It was strangely endearing to me—just like the first time I fell for her—and now, knowing just how easily I'd fallen under the spell of this woman once before.

As I stared at her, I realized I hadn't actually heard her voice since I'd moved back to Stolen Hearts Valley last year. I'd seen her plenty of times—every single time was a yank on the string attached to my heart.

I nodded slowly, waiting for her to flee. After all, that's what she always did when we were anywhere in the same vicinity for the last year.

During the moments I took her in, Grace tucked her arms around her waist again, her shoulders curling inward. She bit the corner of her lip. I wanted to lift my thumb, to smooth the furrow on her brow and cup her cheek.

I didn't realize I had actually done what I was thinking until I was standing right in front of her, my thumb resting over the rapid flutter of her pulse along the side of her neck.

Her breath drew in sharply. I stared into her smoky, gorgeous eyes. I didn't realize I'd been holding my breath until she spoke.

"Boone."

The sound of my name coming from her lips was a fiery jolt to my heart

"Yeah, sugar?"

The endearment slipped out. I could feel

the tension vibrating from Grace, a subtle tremor running through her.

We stood like that, frozen in place with our eyes locked together. Grace's eyes were like one of those afternoons when the sky couldn't decide if it planned to riot with a storm or let the clouds blow by.

Her smoky gaze flashed in shades of silver. All the while, I held my breath.

Just as I had reached up to cup her cheek without thinking, so did I dip my head and brush my lips across hers. Sensation shot through me, so electric was the feel of her lips under mine.

Grace gasped, literally jumping away from me. "I can't!"

Angling my head to the side, I eyed her carefully. "I don't see why not, Grace. I've missed you. So damn much."

She stared at me, her lips parted slightly and her shoulders rising and falling with her rapid breaths.

"How can you say that?" she countered as a look of pure devastation passed over her face. It took all I had not to walk over and pull her into my arms and explain the whole fucking mess. I wanted to make her listen, to make her understand.

Yet, I knew Grace. I knew her *so* well. She

hated to be pushed and only strengthened her defenses when anybody put pressure on her.

Closing my eyes, I took a breath and nodded as I opened them. "Just let me explain what happened."

"Please just go." Her words were raw and frayed around the edges. Her eyes were bright, and I knew I saw the glitter of unshed tears. "Just go," she repeated, this time her voice more forceful.

Wayne took that moment to meow loudly. Mentally wrestling, I debated whether to stay. Just then, my cell phone rang with the distinct warning tone for Stolen Hearts Valley Emergency Response Team. I was on call, and that meant I needed to get going. "I'll go, but I want to try to talk soon. Please."

Grace lifted her chin, the muscles in her jaw tightening. "I don't know what the hell there is to talk about."

I closed the distance between us, cupping her chin lightly. "You know damn well there is. If there wasn't, you wouldn't have managed to avoid getting anywhere near me for most of the year since I came back. I know I fucked up and didn't handle things well, but you never even gave me a chance to explain. I won't take a chance now, but it's coming."

At that, I bent low once more and brushed my lips across hers again, almost craving the hot jolt it gave my system. I recognized the answering flare of desire in Grace's eyes when I lifted my head. Without a word, I walked past her and jogged down the stairs as my phone blared again.

GRACE

I didn't know how long I stood frozen in place with two fingers pressed lightly over my mouth. My lips tingled, and my entire body hummed with a confused sense of emotion ... desire, anger, regret, and so many more feelings I couldn't even label.

Having Boone touch me again felt like two planets colliding in space. My entire cellular composition was attempting to reconfigure and absorb the impact.

Wayne meowed, finally breaking through my frozen state. Dropping my fingers from my lips, I spun around, narrowing my eyes at him. "This is all your fault."

Wayne simply lifted his gray leg and started cleaning himself. I rolled my eyes and turned away, searching out where I had left my phone. Spying it on the kitchen counter, I strode across the room to pick it up. Tapping on my mother's contact, I called her.

She answered on the second ring. "Hey Grace, how're you doing this morning?" she asked in her forever cheerful voice.

I didn't even bother with a greeting. "The property place rented the other side of the duplex to Boone."

My mother was quiet for a moment before asking, "Boone Reeves?"

"Yes, Mom. What other Boone would I be talking about?"

"Just confirming, Grace. Well, I guess you'll finally have to deal with him."

"Deal with what?" I countered, wondering if my brain might explode with frustration at how calm she sounded.

"Boone, and the fact that you've never gotten over him," my mother said, her tone still calm. For a sweet person, and someone I loved, she could sometimes be infuriating.

"Mom, I'm over Boone."

Oh really?

Shut up.

Oh, for God's sake, now I was arguing with myself.

"Okay, if you're over Boone, why are you

so upset that the property manager rented the other side of the duplex to him?"

I decided to ignore this line of questioning. "Is it possible for me to call her and ask her to cancel the lease?"

My mother's sigh filtered through the phone line into my ear. "Hon, anything is possible. But there are laws around that kind of thing. It's not so much the money, but do you really want to turn it into that big of a mess? You hardly ever saw the last tenants there. Between your work schedule and your class schedule, you're extremely busy. I'm sure Boone is just as busy as you."

I bit back a groan. "Mom, that's not the point. I don't want him here."

"Maybe this was meant to happen."

"Oh my God, Mom. Don't give me some kind of spiritual juju bullshit right now," I muttered.

"It's not spiritual juju bullshit. Why don't you come over tonight after you get off work, and I'll do a tarot reading?"

I resisted the urge to throw the phone. "I'll talk to you later, Mom." I hung up abruptly.

Tossing the phone on the counter, I ran my hands through my hair. "This is a fucking disaster."

Restless in my skin, I spun around and ran to jump in the shower. I needed something to erase the feel of Boone's body and his lips touching mine.

Why, oh why, did he have to go and kiss me, but just barely? Why was he saying he missed me?

A scalding hot shower later, I was resigned to the fact that Boone had taken up residence in my brain. There was also nothing more than a single wall separating us.

———

"Grace, I can't come back," Boone said.

I gripped the phone tightly in my hand, feeling a bead of sweat rolling down my spine. I was standing outside in the late summer heat, two weeks into my sophomore year of college.

I could feel the sickening thud of my heart inside my chest, and my stomach twisted tightly. "How come?" I asked, my voice reedy even to my ears.

"Look, I fucked up. But it's not just that. My dad's sick, Grace."

"What do you mean?"

"He just got diagnosed with colon cancer. I need to stay and help take care of him."

I couldn't say why, but I knew Boone wasn't telling me everything.

"Does this mean you're never coming back?"

"I don't know. I'm sorry, Grace. I really am. I have to go." The phone line clicked dead in my ear.

"Boone!"

When I called him back, it just rang and rang, over and over and over again. All I got was his voicemail.

Boone and I had started dating our senior year in high school and had fallen into that crazy, wild kind of love you could have back then — foolish and headlong with enough chemistry to set the world on fire.

Boone's mother lived in Stolen Hearts Valley with his father across the country in Colorado. After our freshman year of college, we decided to take a break. Nothing awful happened, but he planned to stay with his father for the summer and fall. He was taking a semester off to sort things out with his financial aid. We still fancied ourselves in love, but we were going to be apart for five months. We were young, but we thought it would be mature —or something stupid like that—to give ourselves a chance to see if we wanted to date other people.

We had told each other we could date if we wanted, and we could figure out if we really loved each other. It had been my idea. During the ensuing months, I'd gone on one date. All it had shown me was that I missed Boone. About six weeks ago, he'd called and told me he thought it was stupid for us to try to date others.

We had weeks of phone calls and daily texts, and I'd been so looking forward to him coming back. Then, this?

In the ensuing weeks, Boone's silence was complete, and my heart was broken. He didn't return my calls. Total and complete silence.

No one seemed to know anything, at least not my friends. It was only about eight months later that I discovered he had a girlfriend who was pregnant. I'd been so embarrassed to learn he'd lied to me that I told no one. Not even my closest friend, Evie.

I was so torn up over it that I hardly told anyone how much it hurt. I couldn't believe what an idiot I'd been.

———

After my morning encounter with Boone, my day was insanely busy. I staved off one of my brutal migraines with my prescription medicine and picked up an extra shift at Stolen Hearts Lodge, where I worked in the restaurant. I thanked God and the stars above almost every day that, while Boone had moved back to Stolen Hearts Valley, and was on the first responder team with many of my friends, he didn't work at the lodge. I was pleasantly spared the anxiety of running into him almost daily.

I felt a tug on my ponytail as I tossed a load of napkins in the washing machine in the back hallway behind the kitchen at the lodge. Glancing over my shoulder, I found Evie smiling brightly, her blue eyes sparkling. "We're all exhausted, so nachos and wine in the back when you finish up with that last table."

"Sounds like a plan," I replied, trying to inject some cheer into my smile.

After pouring the soap in the washer and hitting start, I hurried back up front to check on the last table in the restaurant. I gave a wave to the line cooks as I passed by. They were well into cleaning up their cooking stations, and the low murmur of their conversation carried on along with the hum of the industrial dishwasher.

———

"Oh my God!" Skylar exclaimed.

I bit back a laugh. "It *is* a good story."

"You are seriously telling me that Lucas got your vibrator by accident. That's how you two got going?" Skylar asked in clarification.

Valentina brushed her red curls off her shoulders and shrugged with a sheepish smile. "Um, yup. That's what got the ball rolling."

Skylar giggled as she paused to scoop a few more nachos onto her plate.

"The only question now is whether you plan to share that story with your children when you have them?" Evie teased.

Valentina laughed. "I don't think so."

"I wish I would meet someone," Skylar offered in between bites.

"Someone will come along when the time is right," Shay said with a smile.

"Okay, so I'm kinda new to hanging out with y'all," Skylar began as she glanced around the table, "but if I have it right, I'm not the only single one left here. You're still single, right?" She turned to look at me, her strawberry blond ponytail bouncing. Her hair was barely long enough for the ponytail, so her wavy locks looked a bit like a sprout on the back of her head. She pushed her glasses up on her nose, her light brown eyes curious behind the lenses.

Skylar was a fairly recent addition at Stolen Hearts Lodge. She actually worked at the vet clinic over by the rescue program. The Lodge was much more than just a restaurant. Jackson Stone had turned his family's old farm into a high-end outdoor resort. He was also a veterinarian, so he ran a vet clinic and a rescue program for a wide variety of animals.

The vet clinic was busy enough that Jackson had hired Skylar as a vet tech to help him stay on top of things. It had taken a few months before Skylar began joining us for girls' nights.

I took a gulp of my wine and nodded. "Yep. Still single and planning to keep it that way."

"Really?" Dani chimed in as she leaned toward the center of the table to snag a few tortilla chips.

Boone flashed through my mind, and I shoved him right back out. "I happen to think single is better. Just because y'all fell madly in love," I said, gesturing amongst Valentina, Shay, Dani, and Evie, "doesn't mean it's for everyone. In fact, research shows that the happiest people are actually single women."

Skylar's smile stretched across her face. "Well, that's handy. I guess I'm on the right track. I'm epically good at finding assholes to date, so it's probably best if I don't even bother."

One of the line cooks happened to come into the staff kitchen to check with Dani about something. Dani, the chef and manager for the lodge restaurant, was rarely off duty. I was relieved for the interruption. The last thing I wanted was to dwell on my single state.

A bit later, after the nachos were gone and there were two empty bottles of wine on the table, our group had broken apart for the night. I was stacking plates to carry them over to the dishwasher. Only Evie and I were left.

When I returned to the large stainless steel table where we'd been seated on stools while we ate, I snagged a clean rag and wet it under the faucet to help her wipe it down. "Surprised you're not hurrying back to Dawson," I commented with a glance in her direction.

Evie finished wiping down her side of the table and paused, resting one hand on the table with a towel held in the other. "He's on call tonight."

I nodded, continuing to circle the towel on the surface of the table. My eyes lifted when I heard her footsteps. Of late, Evie had asked me a few more times about Boone, and

I was relieved she seemed to be leaving the subject alone for tonight.

She tossed her towel in the laundry bin in the corner. Turning back, her voice carried over to me. "I found out something."

"What?" I wiped over the last corner of the table before approaching her.

"Boone's ex-girlfriend never had that baby."

I had just lifted my arm to toss the towel. Her words startled me so much I dropped it on the floor, my eyes whipping up to her face. "What?"

Evie leaned down to scoop up the towel and toss it in the laundry bin before resting her hips against the wall behind her. "I looked it up. Don't be mad at me. I don't know exactly what happened, but there was no baby."

I gave my head a little shake. "But, there were pictures all over social media of her pregnant. I think she was due within a month or two when I found out."

Evie nodded. "Yeah. I did a little social media sleuthing for you. I wanted to know what the hell happened. Boone's been back for almost a year, and he hasn't said a thing about a kid. It didn't add up. I also don't think they were actually together. Even though she posted about Boone, there was nothing that made it seem like they were together. She had a miscarriage. She didn't post about the miscarriage, but her mother did and said the family was devastated."

Emotion slammed into me. I'd been so angry with Boone. So hurt. So embarrassed that all I'd told Evie at the time was that Boone wasn't coming back, and he had a new girlfriend. Evie and I weren't living near each other then, so it had been easier to gloss over it. My pride had been stung so deeply I hadn't been able to bear sharing that he was expecting a baby with his girlfriend.

I barely noticed that I was reaching for something until I felt the cold steel of the metal shelving stand as I curled my hand around it. "Really?" My throat was dry, and I swallowed.

"Really," Evie said, nodding firmly. "Look, I was curious. When we had our little argument a while back when I was teasing you about Boone because I didn't really know how bad things had been, I just left it alone. I wrote him off as a guy who was obviously too stupid to realize how awesome you are. But since he moved back here, I got curious. It didn't make sense that he would come home, and none of us would hear a thing about his kid.”

Looking into my friend's warm blue gaze, I nodded slowly. I'd had the same curiosity. It was just that denial and avoidance were my coping skills for Boone, so I clung to them like a life raft. The life raft might've been leaking and sinking, but I was still clinging to it. It was possible I was stubborn. Maybe.

After a few quiet beats, Evie continued, "Look, I don't know what was supposed to happen for you and Boone. But I know you two are overdue for a reckoning. Maybe you *do* want to be single for the rest of your life, and that's perfectly fine. But it's obvious you have some unresolved issues with Boone. Maybe you should try to talk to him."

Staring at her, I swallowed through the tight knot in my throat. "It's not a big deal," I said hurriedly. "Maybe I didn't tell you about his girlfriend being pregnant back then—and I'm *really* sorry to hear that she had a miscarriage because I'm guessing it was hard—but when all is said and done, it was just a break up. It took me by surprise and hurt my feelings, but it's nothing more than that."

When a lock of hair fell over her eyes, Evie blew a puff of air, effectively sweeping it to the side of her forehead. "If it was nothing more than that, then you wouldn't avoid him so much."

I narrowed my eyes, resting my hand on my hip as I gripped the edge of the metal shelf with my other. "What the hell? Are you on his side now?"

"Oh my God! I'm not on anybody's side but yours. I've hardly talked to Boone. I mean I say "hi" and I'm polite, but that's about it. Dawson says he's a perfectly nice guy. I'm only saying something because it obviously still gets to you. I'm concerned because I care about you."

Guilt struck me as worry filled her eyes, and her brow scrunched up. "I'm sorry. I totally overreacted," I said quickly.

Evie pushed away from the wall, stepping in front of me and sliding a hand over my shoulder with a gentle squeeze. "I know. I'm here for you however you need me. But I think Boone is a giant trigger for you. It'd be nice for *you* if you could neutralize that."

BOONE

The steering wheel slid under my hand as I turned into the parking lot at the medical clinic. Stolen Hearts Valley Emergency Response used a medical clinic in Asheville for annual physicals, and I was due for mine. Although I hadn't been with the Stolen Hearts crew for a full year, my last physical had been over a year ago in Colorado.

Like most men, I avoided the doctor. I figured I could blow this off. Until Nick Hudson, our administrative supervisor, told me to get my ass down here and deal with getting my physical. Pocketing my keys after I parked, I walked into the large medical complex.

Stopping in front of the bank of elevators,

my eyes scanned the row of options, settling on the office number for the clinic listed on the paperwork. Once inside the elevator, I tapped the button for the fourth floor and waited. I counted five people filing off the elevator and another five following me in. Suffice it to say, this was a busy office.

Dr. Hall, as he asked me to call him, was a friendly sort. He made the humiliating experience of being poked and prodded as pleasant and seamless as possible. Standing by the door after it was all over, I caught his eye and winked. "I guess I won't lie. I'll be back next year. You're not too bad for a doctor."

Dr. Hall flashed a quick grin, returning my wink. Spinning in the chair where he sat beside a counter along the wall, he said, "You're fit as a fiddle, as they say. No need to be afraid of doctors."

"Didn't you already give me this lecture?"

"I find repetition doesn't hurt, especially when it comes to men and their irrational fear of doctors," he quipped.

"Gotcha. Well, I'm out of here. You'll send the paperwork wherever it needs to go?"

"I won't personally send it over, but our admin staff will take care of it this afternoon. See you next year."

At that, I departed. As I walked down the cool, sterile hallway, my boots echoed on the tile floor. When I stepped into the waiting area, I scanned the area to find the desk where I'd been directed to check out.

As my eyes landed on the row of chairs in front of the cubicle spaces, my heart gave a funny little catch when I saw Grace there. She was leaning forward, speaking to a woman through the transparent partition. Even from across the room, I could tell she was anxious. Her shoulders were held rigidly, and her hand was curled tightly around a pen. Before I thought about it, I strode quickly across the room, slipping into the chair in the space beside her. Although there was a small divider wall between us — some sort of attempt at creating the impression of privacy — I could hear Grace.

I didn't even give a damn about eavesdropping. I knew from being back in town going on a year now that there were comments and worry about Grace and her headaches. I didn't know what the hell they were about, but maybe I'd find out.

"What do you mean more? Another test?" I heard Grace ask.

Unfortunately for me, all I could hear was the murmur of a reply from the woman on the other side. Just then, a woman slipped into the chair directly across from me. "Hi there," she said with a bright smile. "How can I help you, hon?"

"The lady who checked me in told me not to leave without checking out," I explained.

The woman clicked on a keyboard in front of her, glancing at a screen angled at her side. "Of course she did, and we do appreciate you following instructions. What's your name?"

"Boone Reeves."

She tapped a few keys and looked up with another smile. "You're all set. Your insurance covers this completely. We'll get your paperwork sent over to Stolen Hearts Emergency Response. That's the correct place, right?"

"Sure is, ma'am."

"Just a sec and I'll get you the printout for your records."

She stood, giving me another chance to be nosy. "Okay, so that's in two weeks?" I heard Grace asking.

All I could hear was another murmured reply.

"That's at three o'clock on a Wednesday?" Grace asked.

Mentally filing that detail away, I smiled

when the woman returned and slipped a piece of paper under the window between us.

"Thank you," I said, thinking I'd better skedaddle before Grace realized I was right next to her.

As I stood, so did she. Hell. Oh well, she was my neighbor now, so she might as well get used to seeing me. I didn't know when the time would be right, but I intended to explain just what the hell happened that summer.

Her eyes flashed the moment she saw me, and her lips tightened in a thin line. That was a shame. Because Grace had the sexiest damn mouth I'd ever seen. Her lips were full, plump cushions perfect for kissing with a little dip on the top one that created a per-fect bow shape.

"Hey, Grace."

"Hey, Boone," she replied, looping her purse over her shoulder and holding it tight against her hip. "What are you doing here?" She began walking swiftly across the recep-tion area.

I followed right along. "Annual physical. You?"

"Same," she said. Every word that came out of her mouth was clipped.

I held the door open when we reached it,

savoring the crisp, citrusy scent of her hair as she passed by me. She was too damn polite to tell me to fuck off like I knew she wanted to.

I came to an abrupt conclusion. I'd given Grace plenty of space since I moved back. Although I surmised she had come up with her own version of events about what went down, it was clear giving her space wasn't going to solve any of this.

Once we were outside, I was pretty sure she intended to walk away without saying goodbye. Fat chance of that as far as I was concerned. As fast as Grace could walk, my legs were a hell of a lot longer than hers. Following her straight to her car, I stopped beside her, resting a hand on the hood.

"All right, Grace, you can tell me to fuck off. You can tell me to go to hell, but I'm not going anywhere. For God's sake, just talk to me."

She had her keys in hand when her eyes whipped up to mine. A soft breeze gusted across the parking lot, lifting her hair and spinning it in a little swirl around her shoulders. I saw the slight shiver run through her and had to physically resist the urge to pull her close.

I had epically fucked up, but not the way

Grace thought. I just wanted a chance to make it right.

"Well, I'm standing here talking to you, aren't I?" she countered, her tone just this side of biting.

Although there were plenty of things I wanted to discuss with Grace, namely and most particularly to clear up what I presumed was a massive misunderstanding about that summer, entirely brought on by me. I'd panicked and relied on avoidance as a way to deal with the panic. I'd hurt us both badly in the process.

Foremost in my mind though, was why the hell Grace had another doctor's appointment in two weeks?

"I'm just gonna get right to it, what's up? Why do you have another appointment in two weeks? And why have I heard Shay and Evie mentioning they're worried about your headaches when you call out from work?"

Bright red flagged on Grace's cheeks, followed quickly by her skin paling. I saw her fingers tighten on her keys. Her eyes searched mine for a moment before she looked away toward the mountains.

I gave her a moment because I knew I was pushing my limits here as it was. I allowed myself to absorb the sight of her—the clean, almost sharp lines of her profile. I'd always loved the contrast of Grace. She came across as so buttoned up and uptight, yet when she let her guard down, she was big-hearted and sweet—a juxtaposition of her sharp qualities. She was also feisty as hell. She'd always been the kind of friend who stood up for anyone she cared about.

She turned back to me, and I didn't even bother hiding that I'd been staring at her. The moment I looked into her eyes, I stepped closer. "What is it?"

She swallowed, the tension in her face easing slightly. I could practically see the instant the wheels turned in her brain, and she decided she was going to tell me something.

"I've been getting these migraines. They come and go, and I blew it off, well, for too long." Pausing, she let out a sharp laugh. "Anyway, I finally came in a few weeks ago. They set up this appointment for some tests, and now they set up another appointment."

"Do they know what the hell's going on?" I asked, suddenly wanting to storm back into that doctor's office and demand answers.

She lifted a shoulder in a small shrug. "Um, not really. I guess they want me back for more testing to rule out a seizure disorder."

"Have you ever had a seizure?" I asked, unconsciously stepping closer and catching her hand in mine. I didn't even realize I'd done that until she let go of the death grip on her purse and curled her hand into mine. It was ice cold.

"Grace, you're freezing. Get in the car," I said, turning to reach for the driver's side door.

Her lips kicked up at one corner, her eyes glinting. "You're the one who's got me out here talking. It's not that warm yet, you know. Plus, that office is freezing."

Just then, as bad luck would have it, the emergency ring sounded on my phone.

I looked up about to tell her that I had a few minutes, but she beat me. "You go on, Boone. I don't have anything else to add. You know as much as I know at this point. You've got a drive ahead of you."

To say I was torn didn't quite cut it. When Grace reached past me to open her car door, I decided to take the blessing I'd been granted. She didn't chase me off, she let me touch her, and she told me at least what she knew about what was going on.

I'd be stopping by her place tonight. Seeing as all I had to do was walk over to the other side of the duplex, that was easy.

Chapter Five

BOONE

Wrapping a towel around my waist, I stepped out of the shower area back at the station and crossed into the locker room. Jackson was partially dressed in jeans and was presently rubbing his damp hair with a towel. Glancing over, he said, "Hey, man. Glad you were able to get back in time to help us out."

"Of course," I replied as I stepped to my locker and swung it open. Taking out a clean pair of jeans and a T-shirt, I dropped my towel and got dressed quickly.

As I dressed, Jackson continued talking while he pulled on a T-shirt. "You're a damn good climber. Maybe the best we've got on the crew now."

Walker, who was the most recent addition to the rescue crew, chimed in, "I'll say."

Tossing my towel into the hamper in the corner, I glanced between them as I sat down on the long wooden bench in front of the lockers. "I don't know about that." Looking to Jackson and nudging my chin in his direction, I added, "You're pretty damn good yourself. Today was rough from the rain that blew through. Everything was slick."

"Slick as hell," Walker offered as he sat down across from me. He slid his feet into a pair of battered leather boots.

Jackson's locker clanged as he pushed it shut quickly, his rain jacket gripped in one hand. "I swear, most of our work is dealing with car accidents when people go too damn fast on these mountain roads."

"Well, I'd say most rescue crews everywhere deal with car accidents more than anything," I commented. "Although dealing with them here certainly has its challenges. The mountain roads here are different from those out West. Here, the roads are narrow and winding. Out there, they have more passes that cut straight through the mountains."

Walker nodded in agreement. "Hell yeah. Part of the problem now is these roads were built before there was so much traffic. Just take a look at the cities here compared to the ones out West. Carriage traffic was a bit different."

Jackson chuckled. "Good point." His eyes swung back to me. "But thanks. We needed your help climbing down that cliff. It certainly wasn't something one person could handle."

That emergency call had been for a car accident. Two teenagers ended up in a tangle of brush and kudzu off the steep side of a road, hugging a cliff. Jackson and I had scaled down, carefully, mind you, to get the two kids out safely. The location was bad enough that it would be a bit before they got that car out of there. That part wasn't our problem now. Blessedly, the two impulsive kids were going to be fine. Between the two of them, they had a broken arm, a broken collarbone, and a few nasty bruises and gashes. Not bad considering how things could have gone.

After lacing my boots, I stood, and the three of us walked out together. We'd been the last of our group to get back to the station.

"Wanna grab a drink at Lost Deer Bar?" Walker asked as we stepped outside into the darkness.

The rain had shifted from its abrupt sky

wide-open pouring to a steady drizzle. I was thinking I wanted to get home and see if Grace was around and was about to say "no" when Jackson replied, "Sure. Shay texted me that she was already there with a few of the girls from the lodge."

Although Grace was not specifically mentioned, I knew there was a good chance she'd be there. That meant I'd be there too.

———

Not more than an hour later, I drained my beer as I watched Grace exit the bar, the light glinting off the streak of purple in her hair. After our marginally friendly conversation this afternoon, she had studiously ignored me tonight, reverting right back to the way she'd been since I'd moved back to town.

Dawson's voice came from my side. "Well, I think Grace should get an A-plus for how well she ignores you," he offered with a chuckle.

Glancing to him, I rolled my eyes. "Can't argue with that."

I tried to keep my tone light, but I could instantly tell Dawson noticed something. Much as he teased, I'd come to learn he had a serious side, and he was perceptive as hell. He only chose to let that slip every so often.

"Something tells me you want another shot with her."

Seeing as Dawson was the love of Grace's best friend, I figured it might not hurt to talk to him. Not to mention, I could use some advice.

"Most definitely," I admitted. "The thing is, it's complicated."

"Is it ever *not* complicated?" Dawson drawled, a hint of his usual teasing tone breaking through.

Taking a breath, I nodded. "I suppose not. Grace thinks I dumped her for someone else and got the other woman pregnant. On the surface, I guess that's what happened. It's just not as clear cut as she thinks."

Dawson's eyes widened, and I almost laughed. It was hard to surprise him, but it appeared I had pulled it off. I knew my smile was on the bitter side. "I guess that makes me sound like an asshole. Here's what happened. Grace and I dated in high school and our first year of college. I used to go visit my father every summer in Colorado before he died. I had to sort out some financial aid stuff, so I planned to stay with him through the fall semester. I flat didn't have the money not to. Grace suggested we take a break that summer. It wasn't an ugly break-up or anything. She just thought we were young and should see if we wanted to date anyone else. To make a very long story short, I dated a little bit. Nothing serious with anyone. Turns out, a girl I had sex with got pregnant. I didn't find that out until after Grace and I talked and decided we didn't want to see other people anymore." I paused and shook my head. In hindsight, it was an epic case of bad timing and bad luck. "It was like two months since I'd even talked to the girl, and she called me out of the blue to tell me she was pregnant. Right around the same time, my dad was diagnosed with colon cancer."

Dawson shook his head slowly, his breath coming out in a ragged sigh. "Aw hell, man. That's a fucking mess. What the hell did you do? And, am I missing something and you've got a kid I don't even know about?"

Out of this whole fiasco, that part stung. Badly. "No. She ended up having a miscarriage about six months into her pregnancy. We weren't even together. But I fucking panicked as soon as I found out she was pregnant. I just did. I needed to stay home with my dad because he was pretty sick, and I didn't know how to handle what the hell was going on."

"You didn't explain all this to Grace?"

I shook my head, the regret I'd been carrying like a cold stone in my chest feeling heavier than ever. "Nope. I know better now. But—" I lifted a hand and let it fall as I shrugged. "I was barely twenty years old. Not exactly emotionally mature. I was afraid Grace would freak out, so I just pulled back. I knew I couldn't come back here, not then. Not with my dad sick. I stayed and finished college out there, and my dad died a few weeks after I graduated. In the meantime, the girl who was never my girlfriend had a miscarriage, and that was that."

"Oh."

"That's all ya got for me?" I teased, if only because bitter humor was just about the only way to get through tolerating the memories of that ugly, tangled mess. I hadn't even told him the whole fiasco yet, but enough.

"You wanted advice?" he queried, his tone disbelieving.

"Now I do. Any idea what I should do about Grace?"

Dawson stared at me blankly. "All I got for you is you might as well explain that clusterfuck to her. I'm sorry, man. That sounds really hard."

I eyed him and nodded slowly. "It was. And, I guess you're right. I might as well talk to her." At that, I pushed away from the bar and clapped him on the shoulder. "I'll catch you later." I was done waiting.

Chapter Six

GRACE

The sip of strawberry margarita slid smoothly across my tongue and down my throat. I set the glass down on the counter, glancing over when Wayne meowed from where he sat on the windowsill looking out into the darkness.

"What?" I asked.

Wayne simply meowed again. I surmised he thought he saw something in the dark outside, even though he could barely see. Of course, the vet said his hearing was still going strong, so only he knew what he might've heard. After a moment, he leaped off the windowsill and walked to the door, his tail twitching back and forth as he meowed again.

"Boone's not here," I commented.

I rolled my eyes and glanced away. Ever since Boone had moved into the other side of the duplex, Wayne had taken to lingering by the door. He'd never done that before. Whether I wanted to admit it or not, he appeared to remember Boone, which annoyed me to no end.

I had intended to go to the bar and hang out with the girls tonight, most preferably to unwind with a few drinks. Boone had made an appearance and cramped my style more than was comfortable. As such, I had left early. I hoped no one noticed. I'd come home to make a single margarita.

My mind was jumping tracks between two twisted and tangled trains of thought. What Evie had told me about Boone's apparently ex-girlfriend having a late miscarriage, and my encounter with him this afternoon outside the doctor's office.

Although I had nothing more than a sketch of what might have happened, my heart ached a little for him. I had no idea if he loved that girl. I had no idea if the tragedy of that miscarriage had torn them apart. As betrayed as I'd felt by Boone that summer, it didn't change what I knew about him. I knew it would've hurt him to lose a baby like that.

It was so emotionally confusing to have the scar ripped open on my heart when he came back to Stolen Hearts and to now ache for what he must've gone through. It felt as if I were picking my way through a field of emotional landmines.

After Evie's prodding, I had caved a little today when Boone had insisted on trying to talk to me. Whether I admitted it to myself or not, my attempt to box him out of my life by ignoring him had utterly failed. He took up plenty of space in my thoughts, at this point far more than I wanted.

I had hoped, desperately hoped, to go into the doctor today and find out just what the hell was causing these migraines. There seemed to be no rhythm, no rhyme, nor reason to them. I'd never had a seizure in my life, but they wanted to rule them out because, apparently, my father had a mild seizure disorder. So mild I'd never even known about it when he was alive.

The whole thing scared me a little, enough so that I'd told no one about finally going to see a doctor. Now, I'd gone and told Boone because he caught me at a weak moment. I took another gulp of my margarita just as Wayne meowed and there was a knock on my door.

Thinking the only person it could be was my mother, I stood and crossed the short distance from the kitchen island to the door, speaking as I opened it. "Mom, how many times do I have to tell you..."

Instead of my mother, Boone stood there. My heart—my tricky, unfaithful to me heart—did a little flip. It started beating so hard I imagined it was almost clapping its hands and stomping its feet.

Wayne, also unfaithful to me, wrapped himself around Boone's ankles, his purr loud enough for both of us to hear it.

Boone's dark blond hair was mussed. His mouth hitched at the corner in a lazy grin after a glance down at Wayne. When he looked up, his intent gaze locked on mine.

"I'm not your mom," he said by way of greeting.

"No?" I countered, unable to keep my lips from curling into a smile. I had to bite the insides of my cheeks to keep a giggle from escaping. Boone confused me. Oh so much.

I didn't realize I was simply standing there, staring at him until he spoke again. "May I come in?"

It was *so* not fair that such an innocuous question sounded so damn sexy and dirty coming from his mouth.

Somehow the combination of finally getting close to Boone, our almost kiss, that little nugget of information from Evie — which had muddled all of the stories I'd written in my head and heart about what happened that summer when Boone betrayed me, or so I'd thought — and our brief interaction at the doctor's office this afternoon had shredded my denial about my feelings for him.

Wanting Boone came as easy as breathing to me. I'd tried dating since him and repeatedly found it lacking. Not to mention, I seemed to have a knack for finding assholes. Well, maybe not a knack. The only two guys I'd even entertained something serious with had both been reading a different book than me when it came to relationships. The last one, John, had been the equivalent of grinding sand into the scar left by Boone.

You learn over time that the stories you tell yourself hold the most power. It's not so much whether they're factually true or not. Emotion isn't based in fact or reality. It resides in the nebulous world of the heart, complicated by the push and pull of so many factors beyond our control.

I looked into Boone's familiar gaze — dark, intense, and so warm it almost hurt –

and felt my head nodding. Just as Wayne chimed in with another rumbling purr.

Stepping back from the door and holding it open, I gestured Boone through. "You'll have to deal with Wayne."

Boone's low chuckle sent a hot prickle chasing over my skin as I closed the door behind him. The snick of the lock felt weighted.

Boone knelt down beside Wayne, stroking a single fingertip over the top of Wayne's head. "How are you doing, my man?"

I felt caught in a vortex, spinning back in time. Boone had always spoken to Wayne as though he were an old friend, conversationally and casually. Those afternoons after school when he would stop by usually meant stolen kisses when my parents weren't looking, and Boone teasing me and making me laugh.

I gave my head a shake, taking a moment to let my gaze linger on Boone. He wore jeans, worn and faded, hugging his strong thighs like a soft caress. Battered leather boots and a faded T-shirt that didn't do much to hide his muscled frame completed his look. He glanced up from Wayne, catching me looking at him. I felt the heat flood my cheeks. Oh well. No sense in pretending as if I hadn't been staring at him.

As he straightened, he asked, "Does he still have his favorite bed?"

My heart wobbled. Of course Boone remembered Wayne had a favorite bed. It was over a decade old now, but I still kept it for him. A round, denim covered pillow, that had never been meant to be a cat bed, was Wayne's preferred place to sleep.

"He does," I belatedly replied, pointing toward the couch where the old pillow had fallen to the floor nearby when Wayne jumped down from it. Restless with my nerves jangling, I turned away, calling over my shoulder, "Strawberry margarita?"

"Oh, I get a drink too?" Boone teased.

Rounding the small island, I lifted a shoulder in a shrug as I picked up my margarita to take a healthy swallow. Setting it down, I added, "I make a mean margarita. I cover the bar at the lodge sometimes. Slinging drinks for hours has honed my skills."

"I'll take one."

"Have a seat." I pointed to one of the two stools on the other side of the island.

I was relieved he took me up on my offer, if only because it gave me something to do with my hands. Turning away as he slid his hips onto the stool, I grabbed the pitcher half-filled with crushed ice margarita and a glass out of the cabinet before I filled his and topped mine off.

After I slid the glass across the counter to him, I silently bemoaned the fact that I hadn't thought to keep a stool on this side of the island. If I went over to where Boone was seated only to drag the only empty stool all the way back around to this side, I'd look like an idiot.

I was an adult for God's sake. It was just I didn't entirely trust my body when I was in close proximity to Boone. Heartbreak aside, there had been a perfectly good reason for me to work so damn hard to avoid Boone after he moved back to Stolen Hearts Valley. My heart and body had missed the memo from my mind on all matters pertaining to Boone. I still wanted him. Fiercely.

Rounding the counter, I slipped onto the stool beside him, all too aware that no more than a foot separated us. My body—my disloyal, irrational, and plain stupid body – hummed to life. Boone exhibited an easy strength. He was all low-key but potent masculinity. He was the kind of man who gave off an air of leashed power. You knew, if necessary, he'd roar like a fucking lion and fight for anyone who mattered to him.

His confidence was so absolute there wasn't even a touch of arrogance to it. My Grandma always said arrogant men were a dime a dozen. A man would have to do something else to impress her. She was gone now, but she had adored Boone.

I clung to my icy cold margarita, hoping maybe that might calm me down. No such luck. I felt a bead of sweat roll down the valley between my breasts.

Boone took a swallow of his drink. After a quiet moment, during which I could practically feel the gears in his brain turning, he slid his gaze to mine. The moment he started searching my face, I wanted to look away. I was so unsettled with his closeness and even more unsettled by the tumult and emotion banging around inside of me.

I had tricked myself into believing I had actually gotten over Boone. I had told myself, time and time again, that my anger toward him was because I'd truly loved him once upon a time. I *had* truly loved him. Yet now, it was becoming clear to me that my lingering anger was so powerful because I'd never fallen out of love with him. My anger was my shield, my only defense at facing just how much it hurt to be near him.

You could convince yourself of all kinds of things when you never had to come face-to-face with whatever it was you were trying to avoid.

In my case, that was Boone.

Chapter Seven

GRACE

While my mind was kicking these thoughts around, Boone began talking. "I need to say this before what I say next. I'm not trying to pressure you. I just want you to know the whole story. I also need to say that I'm sorry. There were a lot of things I couldn't control. But I panicked, and that made everything worse."

The moment he started to speak, my focus locked onto him. My heart kicked up to a wild, drumming beat, while anxiety churned in my stomach. Gripping my glass, I lifted it to take another swallow. "Okay." I set my glass back down, releasing it to lace my fingers together.

Boone waited as if he were giving me a

chance to—I didn't know—tell him to shut up and get the hell out of my apartment. "Go on," I urged.

I knew Boone and I had to have a reckoning, as Evie had said. I supposed I'd rather just get it over with. I was tired of the jagged edges of the scars left behind by the way we broke up. I was tired of feeling as if my love had been tossed aside. I was tired of wondering just how much I'd misunderstood. I elected to ignore the tiny clamoring voice of hope shouting deep from within the recesses of my heart.

Boone took a long swallow of his margarita before setting it down and turning to face me. For a moment, I thought he was going to reach for my hand, but he didn't. He rested his palm on the counter, his fingertip idly tracing along where the tile met the glossy wooden edge.

"If you don't mind, I'd like to just get it all out in one shot."

At my jerky nod, he began. "I have one question before I start."

"Okay." I could hardly hear my own voice over the thundering beat of my heart.

"That summer, did you date anyone?"

"Just once or twice. But like I told you, I

realized it was silly for us to take a break. I missed you."

It took *a lot* for me to be honest with him. But if we were going to lay things bare, I figured it was only fair.

Boone nodded sharply. "The reason I asked is because I'm pretty sure you think I lied. I did, but not the way you think. We said we'd take that break, and hell if I know why we did. It was fucking stupid, Grace. All the way up until you called me that day and said you missed me and couldn't wait for me to come back, I went out on the whopping total of three dates. That's it. I hadn't even seen anyone for over a month then. I had sex with one girl. I didn't find out until after you and I talked that she was pregnant. I learned that little bit of news on a Tuesday, and that Friday, my dad was diagnosed with colon cancer."

I knew Boone's father had died. I'd been so sad for him, but we hadn't spoken for years by then. "I'm so sorry about your dad," I whispered.

Boone nodded in acknowledgment but moved along. "Because he was sick, I knew I couldn't come back. Not then. I didn't love that girl. It was just..." He paused and shook his head before taking another gulp of his margarita. "I was only twenty years old, and it was a one night stand. I'd used a condom. To make a really long, shitty story short, I couldn't leave my dad because things didn't look good for him. I knew I wasn't going to get that time back with him. And Diana—that was her name—convinced me I was the father. I wasn't. But I didn't know that 'til later. She had a miscarriage around six months in."

The look of pain that crossed his face was so complete my heart felt as if a knife slashed across the surface of it. I didn't realize I had reached for his hand until his warm grip curled around mine. He gave me a tight squeeze before releasing my hand to lift his drink again. "Yeah. That sucked. Because you see, I thought it was my baby. Maybe I wasn't in love with Diana, and maybe I didn't know what the hell to do because I was too young to know how to handle all the shit that was happening, but I cared. I cared more than a little about that baby, and she died."

"I'm so sorry, Boone. I didn't know," I whispered. While Evie had told me what she'd discovered from her online sleuthing, I hadn't known then. It was excruciating to see the pain in his eyes.

"Of course you didn't know. Because I

didn't tell you. It was just all too damn much. I panicked. I figured the cleanest thing was to just tell you I wasn't coming home, then to man up and deal with the fucking mess I'd made. By the time I learned I wasn't the father, my dad was in his second round of chemotherapy, and it wasn't like I was going anywhere. I didn't find out until almost a year after the miscarriage that I hadn't even been the fucking father. Diana never told me, her mom did. Guess she felt guilty about keeping that secret."

A flash of anger rose inside of me. "Oh my God, she lied about you being the father? It wasn't just that she didn't know for sure?"

Boone nodded, a look of resignation on his face. "Guess she thought I was a better mark as a father than the guy who actually *was* the father. She knew she was pregnant when she was with me. If she'd actually had the baby, I probably would've done the math and figured it out. Her mom said she found out she was pregnant a few days before we went out."

"Oh wow, that sucks," I said, not even knowing how else to respond.

His short laugh held a note of bitterness. "Yeah, it did. The whole thing sucked."

He took another long swallow of his margarita, almost draining it. Looking to me as he set it down, I sensed he was waiting to see what else I might have to say.

"What?"

He lifted a shoulder in a light shrug. "I'm not sure. I just wanted you to know the whole story."

"Why didn't you tell me what happened then?"

My heart felt raw. Part of me was shocked, angry, and hurt on Boone's behalf. And yet, I still carried that old sting of betrayal. I didn't quite know how to turn it around immediately.

"I don't have a good answer to that. I panicked. I knew you'd feel hurt if you knew I had gotten someone pregnant—even though that's not what actually happened. I thought I had to take my lumps and deal with the situation. I was never really *with* her seriously at all. We went on one date. Just one. I guess I thought it was easier if I gave you the chance to move on."

"Jesus, Boone." He thought it was better to let me think the worst? I took a deep breath, trying to calm my galloping pulse.

"Grace, I don't know what was better. I wasn't really thinking anything through. I was completely freaked out, and my dad had cancer. Everything collided. I know I fucked up the way I handled it. I'm sorry I hurt you."

His blunt words somehow actually did make it feel a *little* better. Taking another breath, I shifted gears. Seeing as I didn't quite know how to incorporate the reality of what actually happened with my misunderstanding about it all this time, I needed to let that settle for a bit. "I'm sorry about your dad," I said softly.

"Thanks. That sucked too. He had some time before he got too sick, so I'm glad I was there."

"That was a rough few years for you." I was nothing if not obvious when I wasn't sure what to say. Sigh.

Back when Boone and I dated before, I knew his parents' divorce hadn't been the greatest. He'd been a kid stuck bouncing back and forth between them, like so many kids whose parents didn't stay together. He loved them both. His father had moved for work, which left only the summers and holidays for them to visit. My heart squeezed to think of Boone trying to be there for his dad on his own.

Boone was quiet for a few beats before lifting his glass and draining the last of his drink. After he set it down, his familiar gaze caught mine. "Yeah. Rough is one way to put it. Even though I blew it with you, I'm glad I was there with my dad for his last few years. You don't get a do-over on things like that."

"No, you don't." I hadn't realized I reflexively reached for his hand until he squeezed mine.

He cocked his head to the side, his eyes softening. "So there you have it. The messy truth." His thumb was brushing back and forth across my wrist, right over the sensitive skin on the inside. That tiny strip of skin tingled, little streaks of fire racing up my arm and spinning in pinwheels throughout my entire body. "I missed you. I still miss you."

His blunt, unvarnished words hit me hard, almost stealing my breath. He had no idea how much I'd missed him. Just now, for the first time in years, I could experience that feeling without being angry about it.

Oh, how I had missed Boone!

There was something so exquisitely frustrating about missing a person whom you believe betrayed you. There was a special madness to it.

My words surprised me. They all but elbowed their way out. "I missed you too."

I hadn't meant to let that slip. Oh no. But then, Boone had always had that effect on me

—stripping away my defenses without me even noticing.

Another stroke on the inside of my wrist, and before I realized what he was doing, Boone reached over, curling his free hand around one of the legs on my stool. He slid it closer until my knees bumped his.

Now, he was mere inches away. My heart kicked off on another wild gallop, leaving my breath in the dust. Time with Boone had always had this strange quality, a combination of racing by at a blur and slowing to the speed of molasses pouring.

"Here's the thing," he began, his husky drawl sending heat spinning through my veins. "I want another chance with you, Grace."

My heart was hammering so hard, it wouldn't have surprised me if it flew out of my chest and slammed into him. Hope raised a holy clamor. All this time, I'd been nursing anger and betrayal. I was so accustomed to guarding myself.

Boone made me want to forget all that. He made me want to remember the girl I was once before. Yet, I didn't quite trust it. I didn't quite trust my heart to anyone.

As if he could read my thoughts, he said,

"I know you might not trust me. Just tell me if you want me to go."

As if. The one and only man I'd ever loved was sitting in front of me with his face inches from mine, and his thumb wreaking havoc in my body with nothing more than a subtle brush back and forth on my wrist.

Leaning forward slightly, he lifted his free hand and traced his finger across my brow as he brought his palm down to cup my cheek. All the while, my heart kept on galloping along with hope, flinging wild streamers in the sky.

This time, when his lips pressed against mine, I didn't shove him away. I thought maybe I could let myself have this. It didn't have to mean anything.

Electricity burst through me at the brushing contact. Boone tugged me a little closer between his knees. He angled his head to the side, more fully fitting his mouth over mine. I suddenly felt as if we were diving into a place that was both comforting and terrifying.

Because kissing Boone was a special form of heaven. He'd never been a man to hurry, and he didn't now. His tongue delved down into my mouth with a slick tease against mine. He drew away and dropped a kiss on each corner of my lips, lightly catching my lower lip in his teeth and murmuring my name right before he brought his mouth over mine again.

It might have been years, but I hadn't forgotten how good it felt to kiss Boone. It felt both familiar and new, so intense and overwhelming that I felt caught, tossed asunder on a crashing wave of desire. All the while, he kissed me masterfully, as close to perfect as a kiss could be — a mix of slow and sensual. His touch burned my resistance to ashes.

Before I knew it, I was gasping, arching into him as his palm slid down to cup my nape. I'd convinced myself in the years apart from him that I didn't like it when men tried to take control. The thing was, I had plain forgotten what it felt like to be with someone who demolished all thought and got me so wrapped up with need that everything else fell away.

Boone and I were like the sun and the moon to the earth. Emotion, need, lust and more were a force of gravity forever pulling us together. With a gentle tug on the elastic holding it up, my hair tumbled loose as his lips broke free from mine. He pressed hot, open kisses along the side of my jaw, sending a sweet jolt through me. I was oh-so-ticklish, and the moment he nipped lightly on the side of my neck, I giggled.

At the sound, I became abruptly aware the last time anyone had knocked my guard down this hard had been with Boone.

Chapter Eight

BOONE

The sound of Grace's giggle, and the way she shivered slightly in my arms made me feel like a fist squeezed around my heart. I hadn't forgotten Grace was ticklish. Yet, I had pushed that memory deep into the recesses of my mind, in a closet where the door was kept locked, and I could forget about it.

I loosened my grip on her hair, letting my hands slide down her spine and over the lush curve of her bottom as I tugged her a little closer. I couldn't resist lightly grazing my teeth on the sensitive, sweet-tasting skin on her neck again.

She giggled again, the sound tightening the fist around my heart. Then, she stiffened slightly, and I knew she realized she'd let her guard down.

Back in high school, Grace had been a challenge, one I wanted to win. So proper, so buttoned up. I went to great lengths to break through the guard she kept around herself.

When she stiffened, I lifted my head.

As it was, I knew I had already pushed my luck. In another time and another place, I would've told her to loosen up. Not tonight. Not in this time and place, not when she was giving me the shot I so desperately wanted.

Opening my eyes, I found her eyes open and waiting, yet still hazed with the need I knew was reflected in mine. Although my entire body was screaming to let this keep going, I forced myself—much to my body's dismay—to pump the brakes.

I had spectacularly fucked things up with the way I handled what happened before with Grace. I didn't want to blow it again by rushing ahead.

I'd never fallen out of love with Grace. In fact, the years in between had only solidified the certainty of that awareness. Like that summer, when we tried to tell ourselves we should spend a little time apart had only shown us what we really wanted. The years without her had crystallized just how much she meant to me.

The first few years after we broke up were just a muddle of confusion, fear, and pain as I watched my father get sick and die. In hindsight, I wish he hadn't even tried three rounds of chemo because all they did was make him miserable and ill. It was his choice to make, but I wished we could have known the outcome ahead of time. But then, life never did offer up guarantees.

Tangled up in that weary mix of emotions was the mess with a baby that had never been mine. Hell if I knew why Diana decided I was a better bet than the actual father, but that was what she had done. I hadn't wanted to be with her. She had tried to create the impression we were together when we never were. Not after that one night.

And then, for fuck's sake, I'd grown to care about a baby I believed was mine. Only to have her ripped away in a late miscarriage.

All through it, I was trying to keep my shit together. I felt as if I'd lost my footing on the edge of a cliff and just kept falling. I missed Grace like crazy and wanted to set the record straight. Yet, when all was said and done, I thought it best just to leave her alone and let her move on because I'd made such a mess of it.

Grace and I stared at each other. It almost felt as though there was another presence in the room with us—our intimacy had been jumpstarted back to life with our kiss. Her eyes coasted over my face, her gaze careful and wary. When I felt her body start to soften again, I almost—so fucking close—kissed her again.

A very small voice of sanity somehow got through to me. "We're not going to rush this, Grace," I heard myself saying.

I eased my hand away from her bottom, although I didn't want to. Damn, it felt good to touch her again. She carried herself so tightly. It was easy to forget she was all soft curves that gave under my fingers when she let go.

Lifting my hand, I brushed her hair away from her face, a smile kicking up the corner of my mouth when that streak of purple in her hair glinted from the light above the kitchen counter.

"Purple suits you."

Grace's breath came out in a rush, her cheeks pinkening slightly. "Evie does my hair. She likes to have fun with it. She did a rainbow once," she said, her voice raspy and low.

"Your hair was a rainbow?" I let my fingers slide through her silky locks.

"Not a bright one. It was a subtle shimmer. You could mostly see it when it moved," she explained as she lifted her other hand to demonstrate her point.

Her hair was cut in a long bob, curving at an angle just above her shoulders. She ran her fingers through it, her hair falling in a tumble.

"I'd like to see it. Maybe you can ask her to do it again."

"Just for you?" Her voice sounded slightly surprised, pitching up to a squeak at the end.

Yes, just for me. Please.

I'd give anything to be *that* guy to her.

"Only if you want to," I hedged.

Grace's lashes swept against her cheeks when she looked down, her fingertips tracing a tattoo on my bicep. It was a set of wings, feathering out at the edges.

"When did you get this?"

"The summer after."

"The summer after what?"

Her eyes locked on mine, swirling with questions. Fuck me. She was so damn beautiful. With her lips puffy from our kisses, her cheeks a little flushed, and her tension finally easing, this was the Grace I hadn't seen in years.

"The summer after I didn't come back to Stolen Hearts Valley. You know what it is."

Grace's breath caught in her throat when she looked down again. Her finger traced along the bottom tip of one of the wings. Her eyes whipped to mine. When I saw the doubt flashing there, I added, "To remind me of you. You always loved birds. Remember—"

Grace nodded quickly and cut in. "I remember. The drawing I gave you."

"Yeah. That's what I took to the tattoo artist."

Grace stared at me. Hard. "What?"

"I missed you, Grace. It was a shit year, and I wanted to remember the best parts of my life. When I decided to come back, I told myself if you had found someone else, I wouldn't plead my case. I'm not going to rush you though. It's got to be what you want too."

Grace's mouth fell open before snapping shut as her cheeks flushed a deeper shade of pink. On that note, I decided the time was right for me to take my leave. I reluctantly let my hands slide out of her hair and pushed my stool back, slowly enough that it wasn't abrupt. Being honest, I knew damn well I was trying to give her a chance to reach for me.

For a few beats, she hesitated, her hand tightening on my arm right over where she'd been tracing my tattoo. My heart thudded rapidly in my chest. But then, she stood, looking away. Awkwardness fell over us. I didn't quite know how to handle this. Grace spoke first.

"I'm sorry about what you went through, Boone. With your dad, and everything else." She seemed uncertain how to define the "everything else." I sure as hell didn't know how to explain it easily. How do you summarize a one-night stand turning into an unexpected pregnancy just when you're trying to get back together with the girl you're in love with? Only to later find out that you were never the father to begin with, but only after you went through the emotional pain of a late miscarriage?

Suffice it to say, there was no real easy fucking way to explain all that.

I shook my head slightly. "You don't need to be sorry. Life is messy sometimes."

Grace's eyes searched my face, and I felt suddenly exposed. "No matter how you slice it, it was sad. You didn't sign up for that kind of mess."

I knew then she wasn't speaking just of my father getting cancer and dying. Because no, I certainly hadn't signed up for a one-night stand turning into what it did. Holding her gaze, I nodded. "If there's one thing I know, you can't change the past."

Grace was quiet, and then there was a little sound in the background, and I knew Wayne was moving about in his bed on the windowsill.

"Does this mean I have visiting privileges now?" I asked, attempting to lighten the moment.

Grace bit her lip, and I wanted to kiss her again. "I suppose so."

Dipping my head and exercising more restraint than I knew I had, I pressed a kiss to her cheek. "Goodnight, Grace."

As I walked past her, her voice caught me. "Boone."

When I turned back, she said, "I don't know what this all means, so..."

When I shook my head, her words trailed to a stop. "Just like I said. I'm not going to rush this. Sleep tight, Grace."

I forced myself to turn away and walk through that door, walking all the way down the stairs and up the set of stairs on the other side. I guessed I'd be sleeping in a bedroom immediately opposite hers with only a single wall separating us—probably two-by-four studs, eighteen inches apart, and two pieces of drywall on either side with nothing else but air.

I knew I'd be finding my release with Grace on my mind before I fell asleep.

Only moments later, I lay in my bed. My mind spun on a loop—the feel of Grace's soft, plump lips moving under mine and her sweet body close. The sound of her breath catching in her throat played on repeat. My cock was so hard it ached. It was a cheap substitute, but I knew there was only one way sleep would find me tonight. I curled my fist around my shaft and found a quick, mechanical release.

Hours later, I woke in the darkness with Grace filling my mind. The insistent buzz of my emergency phone punctured the haze of sleep and Grace.

Chapter Nine

GRACE

Days passed in a busy blur. Late winter when spring was on the horizon was a time of stunning beauty in the Blue Ridge Mountains, and tourists poured into the area. The restaurant at Stolen Hearts Lodge had truly found its stride within the last year or so. After Dani hired me, back when the place originally opened a few years ago, she had high hopes. With Jackson scrambling to resurrect his family's old farm into a high-end outdoor resort and more, he'd desperately needed help when he hired her as manager.

In the last year since Shay had come along, things had kicked into high gear. Not only was Jackson in a much more cheerful mood—what with being head over heels in love with Shay—but Shay had taken over with managing the rescue program, the vet clinic, and the reservations for the lodge.

That had given Dani time to really make the restaurant shine. And, shine it did. Dani was a spectacular chef and the best kind of boss. To me, she was more friend than boss, and that was perfectly fine. Waiting tables here and pocketing tons of tips made it possible for me to keep working on my graduate degree in data analytics. I loved data, and I loved studying it. Yet, without finishing my graduate degree, it wouldn't pay me too much. This job made it possible for me to juggle work and classes.

As luck would have it, I was scheduled for three days straight after the evening of **THE KISS**. I'd come to imagine **THE KISS** in all caps and bold in my mind. I needed something to distract me. Because when I wasn't distracted, I was replaying **THE KISS** in my mind on a repeat loop—the feel of Boone's lips, the bold stroke of his tongue, the way he simply took over, his control so complete that I could lose myself for once.

I knew I had a hard time letting go. I was that kind of girl. With kind of flaky parents, much as I adored them, I had always craved a bit more structure, a bit less of the go with the flow attitude.

Like Boone, I knew quite well that things often didn't work out. I, too, had lost my father at a fairly young age and missed him dearly. I didn't know what it meant that both Boone and I had both lost our fathers to cancer. I wasn't quite ready to consider that anything more than coincidence.

Unlike Boone's father, mine had elected not to try chemo beyond the first round, which had been unsuccessful. My father had been all about accepting what came your way. Parts of me respected his attitude, while most of me craved anything to do to take control of difficult situations.

The gift Boone had given me years ago and still seemed to have the ability to do, was taking control and giving me permission to let go. I had always hoped I'd find another man who could give me that same gift, but no such luck so far.

An elbow nudged me in the side, kind of hard.

"What?" My head whipped over my shoulder to find Dani eyeing me, her gaze quizzical. Her unruly brown curls were pulled up into a ponytail, and her snappy brown eyes coasted over my face. "Are you feeling okay?"

I looked down to realize my hands were resting on top of the stack of folded napkins I'd just brought from the laundry up front to put on the shelves in the work area for the wait staff. Glancing back to her, I nodded quickly. "Oh, I'm fine. Sorry, just zoning out."

"You sure?"

I knew she was prodding because I'd had a few migraines strike abruptly in the last few months. Dani was a bit of a mother hen. Actually, "a bit" didn't quite describe it. She was a full-blown, bossy mother hen.

"I'm sure," I insisted, feeling my cheeks heat slightly. It wasn't as if Dani could see into my thoughts and realize I'd been zoning out over Boone. But still.

"Okay. Well, get moving. You know I don't like to nag, but we've got a line at the door waiting, and we need to get some tables moving."

"On it," I said, quickly placing the stack on the shelf and checking the small computer tablet tucked in my apron. "I'll do a loop and see if I can move things along to open up some tables."

Dani was already hurrying away, turning and blowing a kiss over her shoulder. "Thank you!"

See, that was how bad I had it. In the

middle of a shift, at the height of madness during dinner, I was zoning out.

I made it through that busy shift, spinning from one table to the next, and even picking up an hour behind the bar when the bartender had to leave early. It was only when I had collected the tip from my last table and was helping carry a final tray filled with empty dishes to the back that I felt the first ping of one of my dreaded headaches.

I didn't quite know why I was feeling so irrationally private about these headaches. Maybe it was because they scared me a little bit. I didn't like to feel out of control, and when ibuprofen didn't even touch these, it was a bit frightening.

I thanked the stars tonight's headache didn't kick in until the end of my shift. I didn't need Dani to worry any more than she already was, or the rest of my friends. Evie stopped beside me as I was sliding dishes into the rack of the massive industrial size dishwasher in the back of the kitchen.

"Do you want to head out to the bar?" she asked.

"No. I'm pretty tired. Who else is going?"

"Me," Dawson said as he came up behind Evie and looped his arms around her waist, dropping his chin to her shoulder.

My best friend's cheeks went pink with her smile. "Well, we are, and I think a few others."

"Boone will be there," Dawson added as he straightened and stood beside Evie with one arm firmly wrapped around her waist. "I hear you're actually on speaking terms with him now."

I couldn't help but wonder what Boone had said, although I had already admitted as much to Evie. "Where'd you hear that?" I teased in return as another wave of pain throbbed at my temples.

Evie rolled her eyes. "I mentioned to him that y'all might be making peace. That's all I said."

"It's not a secret," I replied with a shrug. Evie didn't know about my crazy hot kiss with Boone. For now, I wanted to keep that little bit to myself. I had told her about my conversation with Boone, finally clarifying everything that happened that summer, but that was it.

"You know Dawson. He just *has* to comment on things," Evie said, elbowing him in the side.

"Hey, I'm all about peace and friendship. Why do you have to go and give me a hard time about it?" he countered.

"Because you tease about everything," Evie countered.

Dawson nodded solemnly, although there was a gleam in his eyes. "Sorry. I do tease about everything."

I laughed softly. "Go have fun. I'm gonna go home. I'm too tired to go out."

———

A short drive later, I cut the engine to my car and pocketed my keys, leaning my head against my seat to take a deep breath. My headache had increased in intensity on the drive home. The pain was now encompassing my entire head and throbbing incessantly.

I took several deep breaths, hoping to get it under control. All I needed to do was walk inside. I had taken one of my migraine pills before I left the lodge to drive home. I had yet to really dial-in on the best time to take those. Sometimes I managed to take them early enough to cut the headache off at the pass, almost like a detour on the highway. Other times, it was too late, and I had to wait a little bit for them to kick in and knock the pain out.

After another deep breath, I straightened and climbed out of my car, taking care to move slowly and not jostle any part of my body too much. Whenever I got one of these, any abrupt motion could send sharp bolts of pain radiating to my head.

I was startled when headlights angled across me, and I stumbled a bit. I froze after I caught my balance, waiting until the pain subsided from that jolt. Looking up, I saw Boone's truck. I couldn't even be frustrated at his presence. I mean, he *did* live here. It was just I hadn't expected him right now and didn't want him to see me like this. I lifted my hand in a wave and turned to walk in, hoping I could get inside and up the stairs before he got out of his truck.

No such luck, but then I supposed that was an unrealistic wish considering how slowly I was moving. As I stood by the door and fumbled to get the key in the lock, my keys slipped from my hand with a loud clatter. I flinched at the sound. Pain blinded me as I leaned forward, just as I heard the sound of Boone's truck door closing.

"Dammit," I muttered to myself, fighting the tears that threatened as I curled my hands around the keys. I really, *really* did not want Boone to see me like this.

Looking down, I tried again to slide the key into the lock. Yet again, it just didn't fit. I held my palm open flat and splayed the keys out, trying to make sure I was using the right key.

"Keys look too much alike," I mumbled to myself.

For about the fourth time, I selected what I thought was the correct key, but my mind was fuzzed with pain. Once again, I couldn't get the key in, and I leaned my head against the door, swallowing a sob.

I felt Boone when he approached behind me. "Are you okay, Grace?" he asked, his hand resting at the base of my neck and sliding down my back in a soothing stroke.

Without even lifting my head from the door, I replied, "My head hurts, and I keep using the wrong key." My words came out almost slurred.

"Jesus, Grace. You do *not* sound okay."

My keys slipped from my hand again, the sound of them hitting the porch making me flinch. "Don't lecture me," I mumbled, finally managing to lift my head from the door.

Opening my eyes, I found Boone's concerned gaze peering into my face. "Sweetheart, you need to get inside and in bed. Should I take you to the doctor?" He brushed my hair away from my face. I became aware of the clammy feel of my skin, if only because his calloused palm was dry and warm against the cold, sticky surface of my face.

"I just need to lay down. I don't need anything else. I took my migraine medication." My words were an effort, but I got them out through gritted teeth.

Boone was quiet, but he nodded quickly, leaning over to scoop up my keys. Whether he used his key or mine, the door magically opened, and then he was walking me up the stairs. He didn't even ask which key to use to open my door. He simply tried a few. In another moment, my door was opening, and he was walking me in.

Wayne greeted us by circling our feet and purring.

"Hey, Wayne," Boone said softly as I felt him sliding my purse off my shoulder and setting it down. Seeing as this side of the duplex was a mirrored layout of his side, Boone obviously knew where the bedroom was and walked me to it, his hand warm on my lower back.

I shuffled over and collapsed on the bed. "Do you need anything?" I heard him asking, his voice sounding distant through the fog of pain clouding my mind.

"Just want to get out of these clothes," I mumbled.

When I attempted to take off my shirt, Boone took over. I couldn't bring myself to care. The thing about migraines was that once they set in, they had a hold of you like a vise.

Boone got me out of my clothes quickly and efficiently. I didn't know how much time passed, but it wasn't much before my bra was blessedly off, along with my black slacks and shoes, and a clean T-shirt fell over my head.

I sighed as I curled up against the pillow, and he pulled the cool sheets over me. My down quilt was soft and light. I felt him tucking it over my shoulders, his weight dipping the mattress beside me as his hand rested on my shoulder.

"I'll check on Wayne and make sure he's good for the night," was the last thing I remembered Boone saying as I tumbled into sleep.

Chapter Ten

BOONE

I sat on the bed, listening as Grace's breathing slowed into the steady rhythm of sleep. I hated seeing her like this. Now, I knew why I'd heard the worried comments from friends. I certainly figured migraines were painful, but witnessing her in this much pain was actually frightening. If there was one thing I knew about Grace, it was that she didn't like to ask for help. That she even let me help at all was a glaring sign of just how much she was hurting.

Once I knew for certain she was asleep, I rose carefully, making sure not to wake her. Then, I walked quietly out into the living room and kitchen area, closing her bedroom door behind me. Wayne eyed me balefully when I returned to the living room. His tail flicked slowly as he walked across the room to leap onto the couch. Pausing beside him, I rubbed my knuckles under his chin and got a little purr in return.

With a long sigh, he rested his head on his favorite pillow and closed his eyes. Crossing into the kitchen, I checked on his food. After getting him fresh water and scouting out his food in the cabinet below the sink, I contemplated what to do.

The smart answer would be to leave and go back to my own place. Surely, she would be fine. But then, I'd never been smart when it came to Grace. I told myself I just wanted to make sure she was okay when she woke up. I told myself I wanted to be here in case she needed anything.

While both of those facts were quite true, more than that, I was simply worried about her. I couldn't bring myself to leave. I toed my shoes off by the door and hung up the jacket I'd tossed on the floor when we came in. I crossed back to Grace's bedroom, quietly opening the door.

I didn't let myself think much as I quickly stripped down to my boxers. Grace's breathing didn't even shift as I slipped under the covers beside her. She let out a soft sigh after a moment and rolled toward me. Her soft body pressed against mine, and she murmured something in her sleep. For a second, I thought she had woken, but she hadn't. I carefully curled my arm around her back as she nestled into my shoulder.

I lay still for a while, savoring every beat of her heart against my ribs and the feel of her in my arms again. I finally fell asleep.

Chapter Eleven

GRACE

I was warm, more relaxed than I could recall feeling in years when my consciousness flickered awake in the darkness. For a moment, I was confused. Then, I realized the body behind me belonged to Boone.

My eyes flew open, staring into the darkness. I was on my side, curled up with him spooned behind me, his knees tucked into mine at the bend. I knew it was Boone because I knew his scent. The way he held me was achingly familiar. His heavy arm was draped over my hip with his palm splayed on my belly.

I took a breath, my mind spinning back to the night before as recollections came in fragments. I recalled my migraine peaking on my drive home from work and dropping my keys again and again before Boone got me inside. I didn't remember much else. My last memory was of him saying something as he tugged the covers over me.

Taking stock, I discovered I was wearing nothing but my panties and a T-shirt. Moving carefully, I lifted the fabric to my nose, inhaling the unmistakable scent. He must've put me in his shirt last night. I couldn't help the curl of my lips in the darkness.

When I shifted slightly again, my hips encountered Boone's quite obvious arousal. His breathing sounded as if he were asleep. A dash of joy spun around my heart to realize I had this affect on him when he wasn't even conscious.

My skin prickled all over, heat pooling low in my belly as I instinctively pressed back against him. My own body told the same tale as his when I felt the slick arousal between my thighs.

My unsuccessful attempts at dating had definitely reinforced one detail—the chemistry I felt with Boone was a far cry from anything else I had experienced.

I shimmied my bottom again and felt it the second Boone came awake. His body tensed slightly, and his abdomen rippled when he took a breath. His palm, which had been relaxed on my belly, stiffened for a few seconds before it softened again.

"Grace." His voice was frayed around the edges, gruff and velvety from sleep.

"Yeah?" I punctuated my question with another wiggle of my hips. I honestly couldn't help it. I hadn't been properly fucked in years. To be quite precise, I hadn't had an orgasm with anyone other than myself and my trusty vibrator since the last time Boone had mapped my body and driven me wild with his hands.

Speaking of hands, his palm shifted, sliding up slightly, just enough to tease the underside of my breast and make me want more, oh-so-much more.

"Are you feeling okay? How's your headache?"

"Gone."

I felt him rise up on his elbow behind me, peering over my shoulder toward the clock on my nightstand. The digital clock read three a.m.

"You sure?" he asked, his palm shifting again to slide up and down my side in a soothing stroke.

The thing was, I didn't want to be

soothed. I knew what I wanted. Or rather, who. Boone.

I knew we had a complicated past, one marked with a rather spectacular misunderstanding and gut-wrenching pain based on said misunderstanding. I didn't quite know if I was ready to trust any man. However, now that I knew the whole story, at least I could try to take care of this.

This being the headlong and fierce desire that swept through me, lighting up and sending that heat pooled in my belly spiraling in hot sparks throughout my entire body.

I rolled onto my back, staying close to Boone. There wasn't much light in my bedroom, just the silvery light from the moon falling through my bedroom window and casting Boone in a pearly, shimmering light.

Looking into his eyes, I nodded. "Of course I'm sure. Once I take my medicine, it usually only takes a few hours."

Boone's concerned gaze coasted over my face as he brushed my tangled hair off my cheeks. I didn't want concern. Although, having his warm gaze encompass me like that made my heart squeeze, emotion jolting me.

I hadn't felt cared for in far too long. Boone had always taken good care of me when we were together. He'd been the kind of boyfriend every girl hoped for—not particularly sweet because that just wasn't his personality, but always making sure I was comfortable, always there to help me if I had a bad day. He was like fire between the sheets.

"I promise," I insisted. I shifted my legs slightly, needing to relieve the ache building to a throb between my thighs.

"Grace—" he began.

I *so* wasn't up for a discussion about this. "I want you," I interjected forcefully.

"I'm not so sure that's a good idea."

Reaching down as I angled toward him, I curled my palm over the hard, hot length of his cock. His breath hissed sharply through his teeth. "You want me too. Don't even try to lie."

Boone's hips arched into my touch, a low groan escaping. He heaved a breath, closing his eyes and opening them as he let it out. The look in his eyes was anguished.

"Grace, I don't know if this is the best idea—"

I stroked my palm up and down his shaft, savoring the hitch in his breath and effectively cutting off his words. "I thought you wanted us to have another shot," I murmured.

"Yeah, but I don't want to screw things up."

"It's just sex," I cajoled, as I gave him another stroke.

"There's no such thing as just sex with you."

My pulse stuttered and lunged ahead as I rolled closer to him, reveling in the feel of his hard muscled chest. I pressed hot, open-mouthed kisses along his jawline.

Enveloped in the haze of darkness, I wanted to lose myself in Boone and remember the fierce simplicity of our connection. While part of me understood his hesitance, in a way, it only reinforced just how much I wanted him. With all that had gone so spectacularly wrong in the aftermath of our bungled and confusing break-up, Boone's return and our tentative reconciliation had shined a bright light on one undeniable fact.

We had never lost the magic, that indescribable ability to drive each other wild by simply being close to each other.

"Grace," Boone murmured my name, almost a plea in his tone.

Letting my head fall back into the pillows, I lifted my hand, tracing along the arch of one of his brows and letting my finger trail down over the clean angle of his cheekbone.

"Boone, I appreciate you trying to be a gentleman. But I haven't been fucked properly in far too long. I know we have things to figure out. But let's not pretend that we don't want each other. That's the one thing we always got right."

My heartbeat was tripping and stumbling over itself, racing along with such force, my breath came in shallow pants.

Boone held my gaze in the silvery moonlight, his look fierce, warm, and encompassing. When he looked at me like that, it felt as if we were the only two people in the whole wide world, as if nothing existed outside of this tiny space holding us within its embrace.

"I never was very good at saying no to you," he said, a little laugh escaping.

Rocking my hips into his arousal, I said, "Make me forget."

In a fiery second, his mouth was on mine, and our kiss went wild instantly—a rough, messy tangle of tongues. Boone's hands, his knowing, strong hands, mapped my body. One slid across the plane of my abdomen to cup my mound, and the other cupped my breast, his thumb teasing back and forth over my peaked nipple through the thin cotton of his T-shirt.

When his lips broke free from mine, I gasped a question. "How did I end up in your T-shirt?"

His mouth was on my neck, sending shivers chasing in its wake as he blazed a trail over the sensitive skin. His lips pressed a hot kiss right at the dip at the base of my throat. I trembled under the feel of his lips moving against my skin as he shifted over me, his tongue trailing down to the valley between my breasts as he dragged the collar of his shirt out of the way.

"You needed something to sleep in, so I gave you my shirt," he rasped when he lifted his head.

Somehow, that simple answer and how straightforward it was—so like Boone—cinched the strings that had frayed between us tighter together. For a moment, my breath caught as the implications of this moment became clear.

He muttered something else before lifting his head. "Time for it to come off."

At his blunt words and the kick of his lips at one corner, the look in his eyes nothing but wicked, my belly fluttered, and my heart thumped rapidly. He splayed one large palm on my belly before leaning back and catching the hem of his T-shirt with the other hand as he tugged it up.

I helpfully lifted my head and arms before tossing the T-shirt to the floor. Boone let out a strangled laugh. "Oh, Grace. You are so fucking beautiful, so fucking sexy."

I felt flushed all over as his eyes swept up and down my body. I couldn't place exactly how long it had been since I'd had sex—it was that distant—but I knew no man had ever made me feel quite the way Boone did. He had this way of making me feel amazing in the dirtiest way possible.

As if to prove my point, his palm slid up, the calloused surface sending streaks of fire over my skin as his touch made its way up to cup a breast. In a flash, he dipped his head, his teeth grazing my nipple as he sucked on it lightly, sending a sharp, piercing jolt of pleasure straight through me.

"Boone!" I gasped.

"Yeah, baby?"

Something about the common endearment slipping through his lips, said just the way only Boone said it, tugged at my heartstrings. It laced me closer and closer to him, and spun me into this shimmering web of intimacy that only he could weave around us.

I didn't even know what he was asking, but I tried to reply, only to have whatever I attempted to say morph into a moan as his tongue swirled around my nipple. He shifted to the other and gave it a hard suck as his palm slid back down over my belly and between my thighs, his fingers teasing over the damp silk there.

"My girl is all wet," he murmured against my skin.

"It's all your fault," I gasped in between moans.

"Missed you, Grace." His mouth was blazing a hot trail over my belly, the slight scrape of his stubble yet another sensation spinning into all the rest as the intensity overtook me.

I barely recognized myself when my hips bumped into his touch as he pressed lightly over my swollen clit through my panties. My words came out broken but true. "Missed—" *Gasp.* "—you—" A sharp cry escaped when he hooked a finger over the edge of my panties and dipped into my slick arousal. "—too."

"Ah, so this is what I gotta do to get the truth out of you."

There was a hint of teasing in his tone, but a wave of emotion crashed through me at his words. Tossed asunder on the tumultuous waves of need rocking me, I didn't even try to deny it.

"Boone..." His name was a broken, ragged plea.

"I got you," he murmured, the motion of his lips on my belly sending goosebumps chasing all over my skin.

I felt his fingers curl over the side of my panties and yank them down my legs. His eyes were dark on mine when he lifted his head, light gilding his broad shoulders as I looked back at him. My heart tumbled wildly, need rushing through me with such force I could hardly breathe.

I knew only one thing. Every beat of my heart was chanting—*Boone, Boone, Boone.*

I felt his palms sliding up my calves to push my knees apart. His lips dusted across the tops of my breasts. There was a swirl of a tongue around a nipple, the graze of his teeth over the other, a few more fiery hot kisses on the sensitive skin on my belly, and then the sweet, piercing pleasure of his fingers sliding into my slick folds.

He sank one finger inside, slow enough to feel like a form of sweet torture. When I cried out, my hips bucked into his hand. Another thick finger joined the first, and then

Boone's mouth came down to further the madness.

Since Boone, I'd come to the conclusion I wasn't the biggest fan of a man going down on me. I'd apparently forgotten just how mind-blowing it could be when it was Boone in charge. He knew just how to do it, his fingers fucking me slowly, his tongue exploring every inch of me—slow licks, light suction on my clit, and I felt stars exploding throughout my entire body.

I lost all sense of time, drifting in an intense pleasure propelling through me again and again. The intensity gathered, a wave curling into itself until I was desperate for it to break loose.

I distantly heard my cries, the frayed sound of my voice as I pleaded with him to give me what I needed. His fingers drove deep just as his tongue swirled around my swollen clit, giving it a little more suction. The wave finally broke, the pressure crashing over me and pulling me under.

Boone stayed with me, not drawing away until my body's shudders were tiny tremors running through me from head to toe. He dusted kisses over my belly as he made his way back up. Every touch felt like a little spark, the heat radiating outward. I started to curl my legs around his hips and pull him into the cradle of mine, but he rolled to my side. One palm rested on my belly with the other brushing my hair away from my face as he propped himself up on an elbow.

It was an effort, but I opened my heavy-lidded eyes. His gaze snagged mine and held it. I languidly lifted a calf, trying to nudge him closer, but he shook his head. "Not tonight."

"Why?" I demanded.

"Because that was already rushing more than I wanted."

Reaching between us, I boldly dragged my palm over his hard arousal, feeling the heat of it through his cotton boxer briefs.

"Not fair," I muttered.

"Oh?" he countered.

"You don't always get to be in control."

Moving swiftly, I rose up, pushing him back and straddling him. Boone's low laugh squeezed my heart. "If you're going to be all bossy and insist we technically don't have sex, then I'm going to do this."

With a saucy grin, I shimmied back quickly, dragging the waistband of his boxers down as I did. His cock sprang free, and I curled my palm around it, the silky skin warm under my touch.

Boone tried to protest. "Grace..." he began, his words trailing off when I dipped my head and swirled my tongue around the tip of his cock.

The salty, tangy flavor of his pre-cum danced over the surface of my tongue. Another swirl, and then I took him in my mouth. If he meant to argue the point, it was lost in a rough groan as I brought him in deep, until his cock bumped the back of my throat.

Chapter Twelve

BOONE

All of my awareness was centered on the feel of Grace's warm, slick mouth, and the gentle suction when she drew me in deep. I meant for this just to be for her, but she yanked the reins of control away from me.

I collapsed into the pillows, one hand fisting her hair and the other the sheets as she drove me to the brink with her naughty mouth. After she dragged her tongue along the underside at one point, dropping wet kisses when she reached the crown, she murmured, "All you have to do is tell me to stop, Boone."

Grace, with that naughty note in her tone and her precise, southern drawl, nearly made me come right then. With an effort, I dragged my eyes open and found hers in the moonlit room.

She paused, her tongue darting out to swirl around the tip of my cock yet again. "You know I can't," I managed on the heels of a ragged breath.

Grace's smile was slow before she sucked me in again. In a fiery second, my release raced through me, coming out in rough spurts as she drank every drop.

———

Daybreak came in fragments—thin light filtering through the sheer curtains in Grace's bedroom windows. A little later, a bright splash of gold across her shoulders when I opened my eyes. The soft rhythm of her breathing, her breath warm on my shoulder. Emotion spun like smoke around me—a piercing sense of regret struck me, along with an immense feeling of relief.

As I had fumbled and stumbled my way through the choices I felt I had to make in the weeks of that fateful summer and autumn that tore me away from Grace, I hadn't known the right thing to do. *At all*. With doubt upon doubt jostling for space in my mind, and my heart firm in its resolution that

I wanted nothing more than to return to North Carolina to be with Grace when life didn't seem to be offering that option, I had simply panicked.

The happiness shimmering on my horizon slipped out of grasp. Just like that. Between my father's diagnosis and Diana lying to me about allegedly being the father of her baby, I'd felt completely cornered. After my father died and I did all the things one has to do after that—a labyrinth of logistics for anyone who loses someone they love —I had known I would always come back to Stolen Hearts Valley. Not only because my mother was here. I'd known I wanted to come back for Grace and to claim the chance that slipped away from us once before.

Although my parents hadn't stayed together, they'd stayed on good terms. My mother had fully supported my decision to stay with my father during those last few years. Once he was gone though and there was nothing left tying me down, I had hoped upon hope I would get a second chance with Grace.

Here she was now, warm and soft beside me. My cock swelled slightly, nudging my awareness. I ignored it. Grace had already pushed me further than I wanted to go.

I wanted to claim her—body, heart, soul. I absolutely did. But I didn't want to blow it, so I had to fight to take it slow.

Grace had never liked being rushed. In fact, the Grace I knew simply dug her heels in if she felt pushed too far. Not that I'd been wondering, but I now knew with certainty our chemistry hadn't lost its spark. If any-thing, it had only strengthened in its force. Yet, I didn't want that to be the thing that brought us together, not that alone.

I heard a slight shuffling sound outside her bedroom door and guessed it was the cat. If there were ever a moment when I did *not* want to get out of bed, it was now.

My body was clamoring for me to stay and slide my hand into the waiting heat I knew I would find between her thighs. But not yet. She needed to know I was solid, and that I wasn't just here because of the fierce need driving me.

If a person could have their own personal force of gravity, Grace was it for me. Getting close to her had just pulled me right in. Now that I'd had a taste of her again—and, holy hell, was that taste sweet and hot—I didn't intend to let go.

Rolling my head to the side, I saw that the clock read six-thirty a.m. No matter what, I needed to get into the station within the hour. We had a few drills to run today and a training session this afternoon. Turning back to Grace, I gave in to the temptation to let my fingers slide through her hair, smiling at the purple streaks. I swept my hand down the silky skin of her back to cup the delectable curve of her bottom.

I dusted a kiss across her lips and was drawing back, sternly ordering myself to climb out of bed and go, when Grace's eyes fluttered open. The second I was caught in her silvery gaze, I couldn't look away.

Her cheeks were pink from sleep. After a quiet moment, she lifted a hand from where it had been resting on my chest and traced along my jaw with her fingertip, the touch tingling over my skin.

"Good morning, Boone," she said, her voice raspy.

"Mornin', sugar. I was just about to get up. How's your head?"

She arched a brow. "Like I told you the last time we were awake, it's fine." Her lips curled with a small smile, but there was a thread of stubbornness in her tone. Lord knows, I wanted to press, but I sure as hell knew now wasn't the time. "I'll make you breakfast," she said next, surprising me.

"You don't—" I began.

"I know I don't have to, Boone," she said, her words clearer now, that tidy pronunciation turning me on. Who knew someone talking could be such a turn on? But then, basically everything Grace did was a turn on.

And so it was that Grace made coffee and scrambled eggs with bacon for breakfast. It was all quite mundane. So ordinary as to be entirely unremarkable. And yet, the time felt so *real*.

With Wayne watching from the windowsill as we ate, I fell a little bit more in love with Grace. Just as I was putting the plates in the dishwasher after Grace shooed me away from the sink where she was scrubbing the pan, there was a sharp knock at her door, and it swung open.

Grace's mother called out as she walked in, "Good morning, darling."

Glancing over my shoulder, I took in the once familiar sight of her mother. I'd seen Colleen a few times since I'd been back to Stolen Hearts Valley, but only in passing. Her long, light brown hair was flecked with gray and tied up in a loose knot on top of her head. She'd stabbed a bright blue chopstick through it.

Colleen gave off a charming hippy-dippy

vibe, with her long flowing dresses and brightly colored clothes. Today, she wore a blue skirt to match the chopstick and a cream colored blouse. She had stopped to greet Wayne and was leaning down and murmuring something to him.

When I glanced over at Grace, her cheeks were stained pink. I sensed she hadn't expected her mother to stop by and was probably doing gymnastics in her brain to try to figure out how to explain my presence.

I wished we had considered this possibility. Colleen had always been the kind of person who just dropped by. At that moment, she looked up, straightening as her eyes landed on Grace before bouncing to me.

"Morning, Mom," Grace said with a smile. "Boone came over for breakfast."

Colleen practically beamed as she crossed the room, leaning her hip against the kitchen island counter. "Isn't that lovely? I knew it was perfect that you ended up renting this place. I've been telling Grace that you two need to move on from that whole—" she paused, circling her hand in the air, "—whatever you want to call it."

"Mom," Grace said, a hint of warning in her tone.

It had occurred to me before that Grace's

tendency to be quite private was almost a re-action to her mother's tendency to be the exact opposite. Colleen wasn't a gossip, but she laid everything out just as it was. She didn't hesitate to walk right up to uncomfort-able topics and examine them.

If Colleen had a reaction to Grace's tone, it didn't show. "I just thought I'd pop in and say good morning. I'm on the way into the bank and the grocery store. Either one of you need anything?"

This was so like Colleen. If needed, I could probably give her a grocery list, and she'd happily get me everything.

Grace rolled her eyes. "Nope. I'm all set. I'm sure Boone is too."

Her mother smiled again. "All right then. Now tell me, what did the doctor say when you went last week?"

"Oh, everything's fine, Mom. Don't even worry about it."

Colleen's face tightened slightly as her eyes narrowed. "I *am* going to worry about it. Those migraines are frightening."

"Mom, I promised I would tell you if there was something to worry about, and I will."

Chapter Thirteen

GRACE

The tray on my shoulder was heavy with plates as I moved through the busy restaurant that evening. After my mother's unannounced visit this morning, she was here for dinner with a friend, her presence dragging my thoughts back to Boone and what she could have interrupted.

Reaching the large table of the family I was serving, I unfolded the tray stand with one hand and deftly eased the tray off my shoulder. I moved on autopilot. Waiting tables was the perfect job to have when you were knee-deep in a doctoral dissertation. Or so I thought. I liked it because it paid the bills and didn't require much thought.

"Okay," I began, "I've got the steak right

here." Holding up the plate, my eyes caught that of the mother who lifted her hand. I quickly began setting down the plates, hurrying away to get another glass of wine after everyone was served.

After I took care of that family, I served another table before checking on my mother and her friend. "How are y'all doing?" I asked, slipping the small computer tablet we used to take orders into my apron pocket.

My mother smiled up at me. "Everything is delicious, but then it always is."

Her friend smiled as well, adding, "You'll have to thank Dani for us. She has done such an incredible job here."

"I'll be sure to let her know. Do y'all need anything else?"

After they glanced at each other, they shook their heads in unison. "I think we're all set. I was just telling Claire that you and Boone finally made amends," my mother said with a pleased nod.

I bit back a groan. Dear God. I didn't think I would ever get used to my mother constantly airing every detail about my life so casually. I thanked the universe for the small favor of her arrival *after* we were fully dressed. I made a mental note to begin to lock my front door, so I could at least buy myself a few minutes when she showed up.

Claire caught my eyes, understanding contained in her gaze. "You don't need to tell me all about it," she said. Close as she was to my mother, she knew my frustrations with my her.

"Good to know," I said, casting a friendly glare in my mother's direction. "We're neighbors now, so, you know, I'm just trying to make peace."

I saw another customer lift a hand. "Duty calls. I need to run and check on that table. I'll drop your check off in a few minutes."

I hurried away and stayed busy for the rest of the evening. After the rush had finally ended and Evie cleaned up after the last group of customers departed, she found me in the laundry room in the back where I was folding a giant load of clean napkins for the morning shift.

The dryer tumbled quietly in the background as I placed one napkin on top of the other. The repetition of the activity was soothing. I also liked the quiet after evenings filled with noise.

Of course, the downside to peace and quiet was Boone strolling into my thoughts almost immediately. He was like my mother in that way. Not that my mother strolled into my thoughts. But she did have a penchant for showing up unannounced.

At that moment, I heard my name and glanced over my shoulder as Evie poked her head around the door into the laundry room. "There you are," she said with a smile. "I don't know about you, but I never had a chance to eat anything tonight. Dani made a fresh loaf of garlic bread with her yummy spinach dip. Want some?"

My stomach chose to answer for me with a loud growl. I laughed. "I was going to say yes, but if you were wondering, I'm starving."

Evie giggled as she leaned over to scoop up the basket filled with napkins and dish-towels beside my feet. "Let's fold them out there while Dani finishes getting everything ready."

I lifted the other basket sitting on top of the washer and carried it as I followed her down the hallway. "Did anyone else stay late?"

Evie's dark ponytail swung back and forth as she shook her head. "Nope, just us." She pushed through the swinging door from the back hallway into the staff kitchen, holding it open with her shoulder as I filed past her. "Even the line cooks are gone. I guess they're headed to Lost Deer Bar."

"They're missing all the fun," I said with a wink as she shifted to walk beside me with the door swinging shut behind us.

"Exactly what I said," Dani called. She was standing over by the ovens running along the back wall. "I just wasn't up for the drive out there. It's been a long day for me."

"Same here," I commented. "Where's Wade?" I set the basket of clean laundry on the stainless steel table running through the center of the kitchen and slipped my hips onto a stool.

Dani opened an oven and peered inside. "He's on call tonight, and he doesn't like to be out and about when that's happening."

"Have you two officially moved in together yet?" I asked as I resumed my folding while Evie sat across the table from me and did the same.

Dani slid a loaf of garlic bread out of the oven onto a large wooden tray. Turning, she grinned in our direction. "We're still sorting that out."

When Dani approached the table, Evie and I shoved the laundry baskets and stacks toward the end of the table.

"I'll grab some plates," I said, standing and hurrying over to the row of shelves above the sinks. Returning a moment later, I set plates in front of each of us while Dani sliced the fresh bread. The scent of butter and garlic wafted up to me, and I sighed. "Oh my God, that smells *so* good."

Dani flashed a grin, brushing a loose brown curl out of her eyes. After she finished slicing the bread, she hurried over to the oven again. She returned with the warm creamy spinach dip that she liked to pair with garlic bread and some sliced meats from the refrigerator.

"Wow," I said when she set the bowl of dip and the plate of meats down in the center of the table. "You're spoiling us tonight."

"That's what friends are for," she teased.

"Wait, we don't have wine!" Evie exclaimed, leaping up and jogging across the kitchen to snag a bottle of wine from the rack under the counter.

We dug in quickly. Once the edge of my hunger was abated with the delicious fare, and I'd made it to my second glass of wine, the amped-up energy unspooled inside of me as I finally relaxed after the busy night.

We joked about a few things as usual before Evie swung her eyes to me, arching a brow. "I'm sure you'll be thrilled to hear that your mother let me know you and Boone have patched things up," she said with air quotes around her last three words.

I laughed softly, finishing off a bite of garlic bread. "I'm surprised she didn't announce it publicly in the restaurant tonight."

"Do tell," Dani said, leaning over to pick up the bottle of wine from the center of the table and top her glass off.

"We're trying to be friendly. Now that he's rented the other side of the duplex, I might as well try to make peace." I felt my cheeks heating and knew my friends were going to know I wasn't giving them the full scoop.

Evie lifted her glass of wine and took a swallow before proving my point for me. "What gives? You're definitely not telling us the whole story."

I sighed. "Okay, okay. We finally talked, and—" I paused, sobering. "Well, the whole situation is a mess." I quickly re-counted what Boone had told me about what happened the summer and fall when he broke up with me long distance.

Dani's mouth fell open. "You mean she lied about the baby being his and never told him? Even after the miscarriage?" she asked, her tone disbelieving, and her eyes wide.

"Wow, that's seriously shitty," Evie said flatly.

"I know, right? It's just awful. And while all that was going on, his father had cancer." I paused, shaking my head. I started to lift my glass of wine, only to realize it was empty. Dani held the bottle aloft, and I stretched my arm across the table for her to fill my glass.

After a sip, I continued, "I guess you could say I didn't really have all the details before."

"How come he didn't say something sooner?" Dani asked. "I get that knowing all of that now changes things, but it's not like he couldn't have said something back then, or right after he moved back here."

"He said he panicked. Honestly, he didn't find out the baby wasn't his until I think, something like a year later. Her mother told him because she felt bad about it."

"Why didn't he explain it to you to begin with though? You two had decided to do whatever you did that summer, so it's not like he did anything wrong," Evie said.

"I know. I don't know that I would've known what to do either. Between thinking he was about to be a father and his own father dealing with cancer, I'm guessing he was overwhelmed."

"So, how are you feeling now?" Evie asked.

My mind skipped a track, taking me right back to the feel of Boone's lips mapping my body and his hands holding me close. A rush of emotion washed through me. "Boone wants another chance."

"Tell us something we don't know," Dani said, cocking her head to the side and laughing softly.

"What, is it that obvious?"

Evie grinned. "To everybody but you, I guess. Maybe if you hadn't been working so hard on ignoring him, you might've noticed."

"Why didn't you say something sooner?"

"I suppose he was trying to give you a little time," Dani said pointedly. "The important part is, what do you want?"

I needed another gulp of wine to answer that. Despite last night, I hadn't really allowed myself to think—beyond reliving just how *hot* last night had been—about what I wanted. Because the pain of losing Boone before had been so acute, guarding against letting myself hope for anything was a well-formed habit.

Habits had also developed around managing my feelings for Boone. Avoidance and denial were hard to shift away from. For so long, I had missed him anyway. Now, I was dizzy with emotion, disoriented, and didn't know how to feel with the blinders falling away.

I let out a shuddering breath and spoke the truth, surprising myself. "I was pissed off at him because I was hurt, and I missed him, and I thought he didn't care. Now, I understand what happened with context, and I guess I might like to see what happens."

Evie absolutely beamed in response, while Dani's smile was a little more careful. Dani, by nature, tended to be more guarded in general, at least when it came to things like this.

"I knew it!" Evie exclaimed.

"Really?" I questioned, angling my head. "Did you really know? Because I didn't even know."

She rolled her eyes. "Okay, fine. Maybe I didn't *know* it, know it. But I sensed we didn't have the whole story about what really went down that summer. Maybe you didn't want to admit it, but I knew you weren't over him. Not after we finally talked about it." Pausing, her gaze sobered. "Look, I'm sorry—"

I shook my head. "You don't need to apologize. We don't know each other's every secret. You were away in college, and I was back here. I was so upset I didn't tell anyone all the details. I was all about acting like it was no big deal."

Evie reached across the table to squeeze my hand.

Dani cast a warm smile between us. "I guess we'll have to see what happens then."

"I think we're on a roll," Evie chimed in.

"A roll?" I queried.

"Yeah. I finally got over myself and admitted I liked Dawson. Shay and Jackson are going strong, and even Dani and Wade finally figured it out," she explained, her voice pitching a bit on Dani's name as she cast a sly grin in her direction. "I think it's totally your turn."

My heart tapped its little feet in a tiny dance of hope. I ignored it and rolled my eyes. "Just because Boone and I might try again doesn't mean it's going to work out."

Dani rolled her eyes hard, just as the back door in the kitchen opened. We all glanced over to find Shay walking in. "Oh, good," she said, a smile gracing her face, although she looked tired with her hair falling loose from her ponytail. "I was hoping you were having an after-closing snack. I totally lost track of time and was up to my neck in numbers, and then Jackson left on a call. That's when I realized I was starving."

"Come on over," Dani said, waving her hand.

Once Shay was settled in with a glass of wine and a few bites of garlic bread, Evie gave her the lowdown on Boone and me before she moved on to dissecting the need for Dani and Wade to actually get over themselves and move in together.

"But I want our own place," Dani protested. "The studio cabins here are nice, but it just feels temporary."

"Well, then get your own damn place," Shay said, moaning aloud after she took another bite of garlic bread.

Another hour passed while we chatted and broke out another bottle of wine. By the time we finished that one, I was more than a little tipsy. Looking around amongst my friends, I asked, "Can I ask any of you to drive me home?"

Whether it was luck or not, at that moment the back door to the kitchen opened, and Wade, Dawson, Jackson, and Boone came tromping in. They carried the scents of cool air and rain. They were also all soaked. Nevertheless, they were brimming with energy, the kind of amped-up adrenaline that came after an emergency.

While my friends' respective loves greeted them, Boone approached me, stopping beside me and leaning his hip against the table.

"You look like you could use a ride," he drawled, his brown gaze coasting over me.

I was tipsy enough not to care about pretending I wasn't happy to see him. Reaching for him, I hooked my index finger in the loop of his belt and tugged him closer. "And you look like just the man to give me one."

Chapter Fourteen

BOONE

When I came to a stop in front of the duplex I shared with Grace, my truck cab was quiet save for the soft sound of Grace's breathing. I cut the engine and glanced over. She had fallen asleep only moments after I started the drive home from Stolen Hearts Lodge.

Her hair had come loose from the knot atop her head with several long strands hanging around her face. Her chin was dipped down to her chest, and her lips were parted. That invisible cord connecting me to Grace tightened.

Climbing out of my truck quietly, I rounded it and bundled her into my arms. She didn't even budge. I surmised it was a combination of the wine on top of a long day at work. When I got to the top of the stairs, I realized I needed her key to get her in her place. I had her purse slung over my shoulder, but it felt strange to dig through it without checking with her.

"Grace," I whispered.

Just when I thought she didn't hear me, she murmured, "Mmm, what?"

"I need your keys. I've got your purse. Is it okay if I look for them?"

Grace tucked her chin against my shoulder, mumbling, "Uh-huh."

With a bit of juggling, I found her keys and carried her inside. Wayne leaped down from the counter, eyeing me as I angled across the living room to the bedroom door. Moments later, I had her stripped down to her underwear, studiously ignoring the sight of her body as I did so. It didn't help matters one bit when Grace came awake.

Before I realized what was happening, her hand gripped the waistband of my jeans. Just the feel of her knuckles brushing against the skin just above my belt sent a jolt of lust through me.

"Come'ere," she mumbled, her words slightly slurred. She hooked her foot around my leg as she tugged me toward her, almost throwing me off balance.

"Not now, Grace," I said, keeping a tight leash on the need digging its sharp claws into me.

"Why not now?" she asked, her tone soft and almost hurt sounding. "I finally admit I want you and now you're being all bossy about it. You're taking my clothes off, so why can't we have some fun?"

I kept my eyes on the wall as I tossed her bra to the side and reached for the T-shirt I'd found. I was torturing myself beyond reason, but I also didn't think it could be comfortable to sleep in a bra. Her breasts bounced as she moved. The sight of her dusky pink nipples in the shadowed light of her bedroom was tempting beyond belief.

I paused, looking down into her upturned face.

Need dug its claws deeper. Her gaze was hazy, and she was quite clearly intoxicated. I was no saint, and Grace and I had certainly had tipsy sex before when we were younger. But it was a hard line for me just now. "Not tonight. You're drunk, Grace."

Her nose wrinkled as her eyes narrowed in on me with something like a glare. Then, she giggled, her leg falling away from its grip around my calf.

"Always a gentleman. Even when I don't

want you to be," she said with another giggle before she tipped backward just as I succeeded in getting a T-shirt over her head.

Straightening, I leaned my head back, actually praying for strength. On the heels of a deep breath, I rounded the bed and pulled the covers back. She made some kind of effort to pull herself up near the pillows with a little assist from me. I kept my eyes far away from anything other than her face as I tugged the covers over her.

"Good night, Grace," I said, brushing her tangled hair back from her face.

Straightening, I began to leave, but her hand caught mine just as I turned away. "Boone."

I reflexively glanced back, to find her eyes had opened again. She'd only caught two of my fingers, but she held on firmly. "Yeah, sugar?"

"Stay with me."

Her words were soft and imploring.

Not a good idea. My rational voice had a swift opinion.

I barely entertained it. The thing was, I didn't want to say no. I wanted to sleep with Grace curled up against me every fucking night for the rest of my life.

"You sure you want me to stay?"

She nodded, squeezing my fingers. "Since you won't do anything else, the least you could do is not leave me alone for the night. I've missed you for too long."

Well, that fucking did it. As if I could say no after that. "Okay."

A little smile curled her lips, and she squeezed my fingers even tighter. When I moved to let go, she didn't budge.

"Sugar, I need you to let go so I can get my clothes off and get in bed."

Her grip loosened, her hand falling to the bed as her lips curled in another smile. "Oh, good."

I stepped out of her bedroom quickly to check on Wayne. I made sure he had fresh food and water before toeing off my shoes by the front door. I was still damp from the heavy rain that passed through while we were out responding to a call for a pair of hikers who'd gotten lost after dusk. When I checked on Grace, she'd fallen asleep again, so I took a moment to step into her shower to wash off the grime from hiking through the rain.

About the only thing dry from my clothes were my boxers, so I slipped into bed in just those. My heart thumped hard when Grace immediately rolled toward me, murmuring something in her sleep as she curled against my side.

I fell asleep, wishing I had pushed a little harder, a little sooner with Grace.

When my consciousness flickered, the first thing I became aware of was the feel of lips dusting across my abdomen. Each kiss was soft and hot, like a drop of lava on my skin with streaks of fire radiating outward. Opening my eyes, slivers of light, that wispy, gray light of dawn, came through the sheer curtains in Grace's bedroom.

"Grace." Her name came out raw, my voice soft around the edges from sleep. She lifted her head, and my heart jolted, just as my already swollen cock hardened.

Fuck me. Grace, with her cheeks slightly flushed and her hair in a loose tousle around her shoulders, gave a sly, sweet, and naughty smile. "Mornin', Boone," she said just as she dipped her head and swirled her tongue around the tip of my cock.

God only knows what I meant to say next. The only thing that came out was a rough groan when her mouth closed over my cock. My hips flexed up into her mouth, and

I tangled a hand in her hair, gripping as she sucked me in deeply. I clung to the edges of sanity, her name coming out through my gritted teeth again.

I felt her tongue swirl along the underside of my length as she drew back and lifted her head. "Yes?"

"Come here," I beckoned, loosening my hand in her hair and tugging her toward me.

She came quickly, rising up and straddling me. My breath came out in a tortured groan at the feel of her slick folds sliding over my cock. I moved swiftly, out of sheer desperation. Shifting quickly, I rolled us to the side, both relieved and painfully frustrated when I lost the feel of her wet pussy teasing my cock.

"Listen —"

Grace put two fingers over my lips, her eyes flashing, almost matching the morning light. "I know. You're gonna tell me you don't want to move too fast. But I want you, and you want me. What's the point in denying ourselves?"

My heartbeat galloped along, hard and fast, as she spoke. "Grace, I just got you back. Maybe. I fucked everything up the last time. I want to get it right this time."

"There are a lot of things we might not

get right, but there *is* one thing we always get quite right." She shimmied closer, dropping hot, open kisses along my collarbone. "Please, Boone."

Well, there was no way in hell I could say no to Grace, not when she said please. With something between a growl and a moan, I pulled her closer, catching her lips with mine. Our kiss spiraled into wildness. My hands were all over her, yanking her T-shirt off, and letting out a groan at the feel of her breasts with her tight little nipples pressing against my skin.

The next time our lips met, we were just *gone*. Hands everywhere, fusing ourselves in every way we could. Once again, I found Grace straddling me against the pillows, halfway sitting up. Just when she rose up and reached between us, her fingers curling around my cock, reality slammed into me.

"Fuck. I need a condom."

Grace stilled, her eyes holding mine. "I don't have any here," she finally whispered.

We held still, nothing but the sound of our ragged breaths filling the room. Grace bit her lip, a hint of vulnerability flashing in her gaze before she spoke. "I'm on birth control, and it's been two years for me. I was tested after the last time."

"I wasn't worried about that," I replied, filing away that detail to ask about later. How the hell Grace stayed single all that time was beyond me. "I know I'm clean because I have to get tested every year for the first responder team. Plus, it's been a while."

I wasn't about to tell her just how long, not yet. Aside from my night with her, it had been since that summer. I'd gotten bitter after the situation of the baby-that-wasn't-mine.

A few beats of quiet ticked by as she stared into my eyes. Then, I felt the kiss of her slick arousal when she eased down slowly over me. She sheathed me in her tight, clenching core. Sinking down completely, she let out a soft little satisfied hum, and my head thudded against the headboard.

"So fucking good," I growled.

She remained still for a few seconds and then rocked her hips slightly before rising up, the slow slide nearly pushing me over the edge. Gripping her hips, I held tight and clung to my control. Her channel was already rippling around me. I'd never forgotten Grace and how it felt to be buried inside of her. I knew her release was already almost there. Reaching between us with one hand, I teased my fingers over her clit.

Her breath broke with a ragged cry. I watched as her head fell back with her breasts pushing forward when she arched, her channel clamping down around me. I finally let go, my release snapping loose and whipping through my body. Sharp pleasure struck me as I poured my release into her.

I was barely conscious as Grace curled against me, tucking her head into my neck when my arms came around her.

Chapter Fifteen

GRACE

Boone held me against his muscled chest. Little aftershocks of pleasure pinged through my body like the sparks of a banked fire. As awareness filtered in, I let my fingertips trail down his chest and over the ridges of his abdomen.

"You got all strong," I murmured into his shoulder.

Boone's low chuckle spun around my heart. "Yeah, I gotta stay in shape for work."

Although my heart was on shaky ground, and certainty wasn't something I allowed myself to even contemplate, just now I wanted to bask in this moment with Boone. So I allowed myself to be hopeful, to be the glass-half-full girl I had once been.

Resting my chin on my hand over his quite well developed pecs, I peered up at him and let myself absorb the sight. With his sun-kissed hair, the gold glinted slightly in this gray morning, as dawn broke through the darkness. His eyes were heavy-lidded. My belly spun when he caught my eyes. His gaze had always been a powerful beam for me. Once I was locked in, there was no getting out.

That was part of why I'd so studiously avoided him before. I knew just how much power he held over my heart, and now I'd gone and given in. I hadn't just given in, I'd taken the leap myself.

Lifting a hand, I smoothed it over his mussed hair. "Tell me, how did you wind up becoming a first responder? I presume that's what you mean when you say work." With a smile, I shifted, patting his hard as a drum abdomen. "I mean, you were in shape before, but this is a whole 'nother level."

He chuckled again. "I started at the volunteer fire department the year after we broke up. After my dad got sick, I was working a part-time job, and I needed to pick up extra hours. I signed on for more training, thinking I'd be able to do something with it after my dad was gone."

There was just the slightest hitch in his voice, and I slid my palm over his heart, holding it still. "I'm so sorry about your dad. I know y'all were close."

Boone lifted a hand and smoothed my hair back, sliding it down to rest between my shoulder blades, his touch a warm anchor. "Yeah. It sucked. You get used to it, you know?" He was speaking about his own father, but I knew precisely what he meant because I'd lost my father too.

There was a slight tightness in my throat. Boone was entirely correct—you did get used to loss. When someone was gone, time was strange. The pain of the loss was fierce at first. I couldn't even say if the pain lessened, or if your heart simply learned to contain it and carry on beating because it had to. Over time, whenever you thought about that pain, the ache lessened in intensity. Occasionally, things happened—like stopping at the gas station where my father always bought me one of those soft, melting kind of mints—when a sharp bolt of pain would strike. Almost as if to remind you it was still there.

Boone gave his head a slight shake. "Anyway. You know the rest. He died, and I did what I intended to do. I finished up my training and snapped up a job out there. I wanted to come right back to you."

I bit my lip. "How come you didn't?"

"Heard you were dating someone," he said simply. "I figured I'd blown it up so badly that maybe I couldn't clean up the mess anyway. If you'd moved on, I didn't want to get in the way."

For some reason, his answer shocked me. I supposed it was the old grooves of thought, so well-established and based on shaky foundations, that Boone had thoroughly moved on. In all that time, it had never once occurred to me to consider he hadn't.

"It was no big thing," I finally said. John, the only guy I'd gotten somewhat serious with, had turned out to be an epic asshole, trying to play me against a woman who was in my graduate program. My pride had suffered, but that was about it.

I elected not to go into all that with Boone. It was a cliché, and I had moved on from that. John had been my rebound, but he wasn't even a fun rebound.

"I figured that out," Boone said softly.

"Were you keeping tabs on me all that time?"

His gaze was somber as he lifted a shoulder in a small shrug. "I tried not to after a while. At first, I just tried to block the whole mess out."

"I know all about denial. You might call me an expert."

He chuckled. "So, no, I didn't start keeping tabs until I had a shot of coming home. That was only about a year and a half ago. My mom didn't know what happened with you, but she knew you weren't dating anybody. I always planned to come home anyway. After my dad died, I didn't have anything holding me down there. I stayed at my job until something opened up here. Enough about me, tell me about you. I know you're working on your doctorate."

"Yeah, it's in data analysis. You know how much I love that kind of thing." At his nod, I delved a bit deeper into the details, relishing the chance to just talk about normal stuff with him.

"Why'd you wait so long to try to talk to me?" I asked after we had covered the mundane details of our lives. This question had been hovering in my thoughts for days.

Boone's fingers were still stroking through the ends of my hair, and his hand ceased its movement at my question. After a moment, he shrugged. "I'm not totally sure. I think you might agree you were pretty pissed off and didn't want to talk to me. I guess I thought maybe if I gave you some time, you'd cool down. I know you don't appreciate pressure."

"Yeah, but if I'd known the whole story, well, maybe I might not have been so pissed off," I said, a little sheepishly.

"Right, but I still fucked up. I thought maybe you'd come around. It took rescuing Wayne. Guess I should thank him." His shoulders shook slightly with his laugh.

I giggled. "He won't even appreciate it."

An insistent, buzzing from the nightstand broke into the moment. Boone shifted sideways quickly, his abs rippling as he reached for the phone. Glancing at the screen, he looked up after a second. "Gotta go, baby."

I climbed out of bed with him, snagging my robe off the hook on the bathroom door as he hurried in.

"Damn," he muttered. "I need to run over to my place and grab some clean clothes."

Peering into the bathroom, I saw his still-damp work pants and T-shirt draped over the edge over the tub. "I'll make coffee." When he looked up, I added, "I'll unlock the door upstairs."

Boone looked slightly confused. I grinned. "There's a door at the back of the closet in your entryway upstairs. It connects to my side."

A slow grin unfurled. "Damn, I know I'm getting somewhere if you gave that up," he teased as he followed me out into the living room.

Striding to the junk drawer at the end of the kitchen island, I fished out the key and stepped out into the entryway. "Got anything in your closet?" I asked as I fit the key in the lock.

"Not a damn thing, actually. In case you missed it, I only moved in a few weeks ago."

"Well, that's convenient. Otherwise, you'd be climbing through it."

When I opened the door, Boone looked through. "Smart," he said, scanning both sides of the divider door. Back when my parents decided to keep this duplex to use for extra income, my father put drywall up and painted each side of the door so it matched the inside of the closets. It was a handy option, but the tenants didn't know about it unless he chose to tell them.

"You got time for coffee?" I asked as Boone stepped through, wearing nothing more than his boxers. I couldn't help but admire his muscled back as he rested a hand on the door frame and glanced back to me.

"It'll have to be quick, but if you can have it ready in a few minutes, I would love some."

"On it."

I couldn't help but smile to myself as I hurried to start the coffee. There was something way too good about the mundane task. It was all because it was for Boone.

Chapter Sixteen

BOONE

I trudged through the automatic doors at the grocery store, weary and cold to my bones. The call this morning had resulted in a long and grueling day for our team. Because the Blue Ridge Mountains weren't crazy cold, sometimes fools decided to go hiking when the weather wasn't ideal. We were hovering in the confusing time of late winter and almost spring when some days were warm, while others were cool. Nights often dipped below freezing at higher elevations during this time of year, and snow and ice still covered the higher peaks.

What some people didn't quite realize was that, in some ways, the more even tempered climate of the mountains down South could make it dangerous especially when spring was teasing its arrival. Add in precipitation, and the risks increased. It wasn't unusual for abundant rains to overlap with the last gasps of winter as spring approached.

Hypothermia could occur at less brutally cold temperatures precisely because people were tricked into thinking it was safer. Thus, our crew was called out frequently to rescue hikers who weren't prepared. Today, we had fanned out over the mountain to find the couple who needed help. They had made a distress call and proceeded to lose their phone after that. It had taken hours to locate them.

The guy had broken his ankle, and his girlfriend hadn't been able to support him walking out. We finally located them and spent the rest of the day in the miserable damp weather getting them safely out. I was cold to the bone, tired as hell, and starving.

I knew I didn't have much of anything in my fridge at home. I was also in desperate need of a hot shower and some clean clothes.

Snagging a basket, I barely looked up as I aimed straight for the deli at the back of the store. They had damn good pizza there. I also snagged some ham and cheese rolls to heat up in the morning for breakfast. Just as I was turning away to walk toward the registers, I heard my name.

Glancing over my shoulder, I found Grace's mother standing there. "Oh hi, Colleen. Just grabbing some dinner."

She smiled. "Are you having dinner with Grace?"

I bit back a laugh, smiling slightly as I shook my head. "No, ma'am. Good to see you though."

Her wide smile faded, and she stepped a little closer. "Can you do me a favor?"

"Of course," I replied automatically, not even considering what she might ask me.

"Keep an eye on Grace. She gets these headaches, and they've been getting worse. She doesn't like me to worry, so I know she won't tell me a darn thing."

A light-hearted moment had gotten serious awful quick. I hadn't forgotten about Grace's upcoming doctor's appointment. In fact, I knew it was tomorrow and planned to try to sweet-talk her into letting me go with her. I wasn't about to let that slip to her mother, not without knowing what Grace had told her.

"Grace mentioned she's had some issues with migraines. Is it anything serious?" I figured I might as well prod for some info while I had the chance.

Colleen shrugged, the concern on her face evident. "She doesn't like to talk about it. I told her she should see a doctor because her father had a mild seizure disorder and sometimes got migraines."

"Is that something she needs to worry about?" I asked in return, concern tightening its screws inside.

"It's perfectly manageable. If that's what it is. With you next door, I figured I might as well ask you to keep an eye on her."

"Of course I will."

As I spoke, I internally cringed. Grace would be furious if she thought her mother was having me check up on her and report back.

Colleen pursed her lips. "You know how private Grace is, Boone. You don't need to snoop for me. Just make sure she's okay."

Uncertain what else to say, I simply nodded. "Of course. If you don't mind, I need to get going. It's been a long day, and I could seriously use a hot shower about now."

Colleen smiled softly, reaching out to squeeze my shoulder. "You hurry along. I'm so glad you came back to Stolen Hearts Valley."

At that, she winked and walked down the next aisle. After I checked out and returned to the duplex, a shaft of disappointment struck me when Grace's car wasn't there. Although I had definitely broken through some of her defenses—what with her letting me know how to cross from my place to hers upstairs—it wasn't as if I was privy to her work schedule just yet. I told myself I wouldn't have been great company tonight anyway.

After a blessedly hot shower and some food, I crashed. Grace still hadn't returned, and I told myself it was ridiculous to try to wait up for her. Weary, I fell into a deep sleep, only waking the following morning when sunlight splashed across the foot of my bed.

I rolled up quickly, suddenly remembering today was the day for Grace's follow up appointment. Glancing at the clock on my phone, I saw it was only seven-thirty a.m. I knew her appointment was in three hours and hoped she was home. Standing, I walked to the window in my bedroom, which looked out over the driveway. Grace's small hybrid hatchback was parked beside my truck.

After a shower to wake me up, I contemplated whether I should knock on her door or wait. Patience wasn't always one of my virtues. I quickly made coffee and filled two mugs. I added a dash of cream to hers because I knew she liked it that way.

Slipping through the door between the two landings upstairs, I knocked on Grace's door. I heard a meow and smiled to myself, figuring Wayne had heard my knock. Just when I was beginning to wonder if I'd been presumptuous in thinking Grace was awake because she'd always been a morning person, I heard the sound of footsteps.

The door swung open. My heart gave a resounding kick at the sight of Grace. Her hair fell in a messy tousle around her shoulders, and her gray eyes flashed silver with her smile. "Oh. I thought you were my mom," she explained. Her eyes fell to the two mugs of coffee in my hands. "Is one of those for me?"

"Sure is," I drawled, holding one out.

I could see her considering and didn't realize I'd been holding my breath until she reached her hand forward to accept the mug. My breath came out in a relieved sigh. Her fingers brushed mine, sending a little jolt of electricity spinning through me.

"Come on in," she said as Wayne meowed again and approached me, his tail wrapping around my calves as I stepped inside.

"Hey, buddy," I said, leaning over to rub my knuckles under his chin.

Grace was wearing a faded T-shirt over a pair of sweatpants that hung low on her hips. She didn't have a lick of make-up on and had clearly only gotten out of bed a few minutes ago. She was beautiful and everything I wanted.

"I was just about to start coffee," she said with a glance over her shoulder as she walked toward the kitchen island. "Your timing was perfect."

"I was awake, so I figured I'd stop by." When she paused beside the kitchen counter, turning and resting her hip against it, I stepped closer, giving in to the urge to kiss her.

Her lips were warm and soft. I let my tongue tease with hers for a moment before drawing back. "Good mornin'," I murmured.

Grace's eyes searched my face, a slight smile curling her lips. "Good morning, Boone. Should I make some breakfast?"

"That's not why I came over. I just wanted to see you."

Her cheeks stained pink, and she lifted her coffee to take a sip. "Okay, but I can still make breakfast."

"You know I'll never say no to food," I replied with a chuckle.

Grace stepped back to round the island and set her coffee on the counter. "Scrambled eggs?" she asked over her shoulder as she opened the refrigerator to peer inside.

"Whatever you make will be delicious."

She shooed me away from helping much, although she did let me shred the cheese. Once we were cleaning up, I decided I'd better broach the topic about her appointment, or I'd lose my chance.

"Let me drive you to your appointment today."

I was rinsing plates and handing them to Grace as she put them in the dishwasher. Her eyes whipped up to mine, widening slightly. "How did you know I had an appointment today?"

"I heard you schedule it because I was right beside you when I was checking out."

Grace closed the dishwasher, the little click of the latch loud in the small kitchen. She caught the hem of her T-shirt, rubbing the fabric back and forth between her fingers. I waited quietly. Pressure was not a good move at the moment. As it was, I had overstepped my bounds to begin with.

"If you want to. But you're not coming

in," Grace said pointedly as she narrowed her eyes at me.

"Understood." I was going to take this as the win it was.

Grace and I had a brief stare down when we walked out to our vehicles, after Grace showered and got ready to go. She had her keys in hand and stopped in front of her car as I walked past it, pausing beside my truck. Cocking her head to the side, one brow flew up. "Did you think you were driving?"

Stopping in my tracks, I turned and rested a hand on the hood of my truck. I took a beat, holding her gaze as I tried to assess just how cranky she might get about that assumption. Fuck it.

"Yeah, sweetheart, I did."

Grace flipped a key back and forth in her hand, her gaze considering. Although I knew I needed to play my cards just right to earn her trust again, I wasn't going to be anything other than the man I was. After a long moment, she huffed a laugh and rolled her eyes.

"Of course. You're such a man," she said, her feet crunching on the gravel as she closed the distance between us.

"In case you missed it, I *am* a man."

I beat her to the passenger door and opened it. She bit her lip, casting a faux glare in my direction as she climbed in. I waited until she was seated before closing the door, rounding the truck and climbing in just as she was buckling her seatbelt.

"I'm surprised you didn't buckle my seatbelt for me," she murmured.

I tapped the start button on my dash before glancing her way. "Grace, I've never buckled any woman's seatbelt."

"But you just *have* to get the door."

Joy spread through my chest at the teasing gleam in her eyes.

"I don't have to get the door. I hold the door for men too. It's called manners."

She laughed. "Fine. So you have manners."

We started the drive with mist rising above the mountains as I drove. The Blue Ridge Mountains were beautiful any time of day during any season, but mornings in late winter and early spring were particularly beautiful. While the silvery-blue mist glittered as the sun rose like gold in the sky, Grace commandeered the radio, selecting the same station she used to love back in high school—a 70's station. When my gaze slid sideways, it snagged with hers, a shimmer of awareness and electricity passing between us.

We were about halfway through the drive when I figured I might as well tell her about her mother's concern. I didn't know if it was the best idea, but one thing I did know was I didn't want to fuck things up between us by keeping quiet over something.

"Ran into your mom last night," I commented just as a new song started.

I didn't even have to look at Grace to know she tensed immediately. "Where?" That single word question came out sharp.

"At the grocery store. She's worried about your headaches."

"I don't get them that often," Grace protested.

"If you don't mind me asking –"

Grace cut in. "What if I *do* mind?"

Oh fuck. Risking a glance sideways, I saw the set of her chin and the silver flash in her eyes. I forged ahead anyway. "Grace, anyone who cares about you might worry. Maybe it's nothing, maybe it's just migraines. Those are something people deal with all the time."

Her breath was audible as she let it out. "I know. I just don't like anyone fussing about it," she muttered.

Reaching across the console, I caught her hand in mine, relieved when she didn't pull away. Her fingers laced with mine, and the tension clamped around my chest eased slightly.

"Grace, my biggest mistake before was panicking and not letting you know what was going on, or how I really felt. I might drive you a little bit crazy because I'm damn sure not gonna let that happen again. I know you don't like it, but I'm worried. Your mom specifically told me I didn't need to report back."

"Of course she did," Grace grumbled. "She's so damn nosy."

"She is. I won't argue that point. But I'd rather tell you she tried to talk to me than keep it a secret."

"I appreciate that." Grace's tone wasn't too irritated, and I sensed she had decided to direct her ire at her mother rather than me.

"So now that we got that out of the way, mind telling me when the headaches started? I can't even remember if you ever had a single headache back when we were together before."

"That's the thing, I hardly ever get headaches. I still don't. It's just that when I do, they are god-awful. As for when they started, I can't remember the first one, but the first time I had to call off work was about a year and a half ago. They're like maybe once every other month or so. Nobody would even notice if they weren't so awful."

I recalled her ashen skin and the sheer exhaustion from tolerating the pain I had seen reflected on her face that night when I found her fumbling with her keys.

"I know it pisses you off that I eavesdropped—"

"It does," Grace said forcefully.

I squeezed her hand and took an opportunity. "Go ahead and be pissed off."

When I glanced sideways, Grace rolled her eyes so hard they were at risk of rolling out of the sockets.

"I'm obviously no expert on headaches, but after being with my father through his diagnosis, I know doctors tend to rule out all kinds of things before they settle on anything. Do you know what they've ruled out so far?"

"They were checking for allergies at my first appointment. I'm told that migraines are not all that unusual. I guess because a history of mild seizures runs in my father's family, they want to do some tests for that. Even though I've never had a seizure in my life."

"Your mom mentioned that."

"Shocking," Grace said, her tone dry as chalk.

Chapter Seventeen

GRACE

The nurse leaned over me, placing a blanket over my legs. "I need a blanket for this?" I asked.

She smiled as she looked up and pushed her glasses up the bridge of her nose. "Well, if you're not cold yet, you will be. These rooms are freezing."

"Oh, okay. How long will this take?"

Turning away, she tapped on a few keys on the laptop on a rolling computer stand with a stool attached. With her eyes on the screen, she replied, "It depends."

"Will I be able to get my results today?"

She looked my way finally. "If Dr. Canton is available when we're done, yes."

"You won't be able to tell me?"

Her mouth twisted to the side. "Sorry, but no. We're not supposed to interpret the results."

"Even if you have an opinion?"

She smiled. "Even if I have an opinion."

I took a deep breath, letting it out with a sigh. "I sure hope Dr. Canton is available."

"She's definitely here, and she told us to come get her when we're done. The only thing that might interfere is if an emergency comes up. That's why we can't make any promises."

She leaned her hips against the stool, her eyes looking to the clock situated above the door, almost in line with my feet where I lay on the cool table. Angling my head back, I eyed the round tube I was about to enter.

I was starting to fret inside, worrying that Boone had somewhere he needed to be. I hadn't even thought to ask him if he needed to go to work or had anywhere else to be. Rolling my head to the side, I asked the nurse, "Is it possible somebody could check with my friend? I just realized that I don't know if he needs to be back at a certain time, and I have no idea how long this might take."

"Of course. I'll go check with the receptionist right now."

"That'd be great. Thanks."

After she disappeared from the room, my mind started to squirrel about, grabbing little things to be anxious about, like whether I'd remembered to schedule Wayne's annual vet appointment. That was a better option than worrying about brain cancer. I refused to vocalize that fear out loud out of superstition that would make it come to fruition.

My mind spun to the drive here with Boone. After his cautious questions, I turned the radio up and told him I wanted to be distracted. He went along with it, even belting out one of our old favorite songs with me.

I was smiling to myself when the nurse returned. "I spoke to him personally because the receptionist was on the phone. He said to stop worrying about it, he can wait as long as you need him to wait. And honey," she said, her brows hitching up, "your boyfriend is definitely easy on the eyes."

I opened my mouth to explain he wasn't exactly my boyfriend, but thought better of it. I didn't need to be getting into details about Boone right before I had my head examined. Literally.

"He is pretty handsome, huh?"

"Oh yes. But better than that, he clearly cares about you. He's all worried."

My heart skipped a few beats, and I felt a

smile blooming straight from the center of my chest. Boone was stripping away all of my defenses, and most of me wanted to just tumble into it. And yet, it made me so nervous. He had panicked once before and look how that went.

Fortunately, or not, the door swung open, and a man entered the room. He wore a white coat with short dark hair trimmed close to his head. The nurse gestured to him. "This is Dan. He's our MRI tech."

Dan was way too cheerful for my mood, casting a blinding smile in my direction. His teeth were perfectly straight and extremely white. "You must be Grace," he began. "How are you feeling today?"

"Fine," I replied. "Can we just do this?"

I heard the nurse snort slightly, but she bit back a laugh, turning to look at the computer screen.

"We sure can. All right, I'm sure Sally already reviewed everything, but we're going to slide you into the MRI. You'll hear some clicking sounds while the machine does its work."

I nodded. "Yep, she told me everything."

Cheerful Dan nodded and got to work. Once I was in there, the rhythmic pinging sounded as described. I was relieved the nurse had gotten me a blanket. It was a bit chilly in there. Afterward, I walked down the hallway, and Sally assured me Dr. Canton would be checking with me shortly.

Walking out into the waiting area, my eyes landed on Boone. He might as well have been an actual magnet for me. The moment I saw him with a magazine in his lap as he flipped through the pages with one hand, my heart practically started cheering, each beat an enthusiastic clap.

As though Boone sensed I was there, his head lifted, and his eyes locked with mine from across the room. No matter how many times I tried to tell myself I'd gotten over Boone, I *so* totally hadn't. The instant our eyes met, the rest of the room fell away. It didn't matter that this was a crowded waiting area in a medical clinic. It didn't matter that there was a baby crying in the corner with a mother rocking her and trying to shush her. It didn't matter that there was an elderly couple complaining about how long the wait was for their appointment.

The only thing that mattered was Boone. His brown eyes held mine, and he set the magazine aside, standing when I stopped in front of him. He reached for my hand, catching one in his.

"Babe, you're freezing," he said.

Before I realized what was happening, he folded me into his arms. He was warm and strong and smelled clean, like fresh laundry and soap. A hint of his musky scent broke through, and I tucked my head against his shoulder, just breathing him in.

"It was cold in there," I murmured into his chest.

"Grace?" a voice called from the front of the waiting area.

Boone loosened his arms as I turned to look over my shoulder. The doctor stood there, smiling, her eyes bouncing curiously from me to Boone and back.

This was only my second appointment, but I had instantly discovered I didn't like being here alone. My tendency to ruminate didn't help matters at all.

"Want to come back with me?" I asked as I peered up at him.

"You sure?" His familiar gaze searched mine. It was almost laughable now how hard I had worked to completely ignore him for close to a year. I could be stubborn.

"I'm sure."

Boone's hand slid down my spine in a warm pass, coming to rest at the curve of my waist. For a moment, I was stuck in place.

Which made no sense. I mean, we were in a doctor's office for crying out loud. With an audience.

It felt so good to have Boone right here with his arm encompassing me just enough to keep me in the orbit of *us*. Back when we had been together before, Boone had always been an affectionate guy, pretty handsy in fact. More than once, we'd gotten caught making out by my parents, or his mother. Nothing too scandalous, just kisses. Boone always took it in stride and even tolerated my father's lectures.

"You ready?" His question came right by my ear, his voice low.

The sound of his gruff voice and the soft feathering of his breath just beside my neck sent a hot shiver chasing down that side of my body and goosebumps prickling over the surface of my skin.

"Oh! Yes." With a little nudge of his palm, I began walking quickly across the room.

Dr. Canton's curious eyes flicked from me to Boone when we reached her. "Come on back," she said with a smile as she held the door and gestured us through.

Moments later, we were in her office. Looking at me, she said, "I presume you're comfortable having him present."

"Oh yes. This is Boone. Boone Reeves."

Dr. Canton smiled politely at Boone. "Nice to meet you." Looking back in my direction, she added, "All I have is good news."

My stomach still churned, and I managed to nod. "Okay?"

"We've ruled out all potential significant concerns. I think it's one of two things. You could simply be susceptible to migraines. That happens. It's unfortunate, and they're miserable, but that may be all it is."

Impatient, I jumped in. "Well, what's the other thing?"

"I'm recommending you have a chat with your OB/GYN. You're taking oral contraceptives, correct?"

I felt suddenly self-conscious. I mean, here we were discussing my birth control. With the doctor. In front of Boone.

"Um, yes."

"Well, a potential side effect of some oral contraceptives is migraines."

Staring at her, my mouth fell open. "Do you mean I can't take birth control?"

Dr. Canton shook her head. "No. That's not what I'm saying. I'm suggesting you talk with your OB/GYN and try a different variation. There are many options, including an IUD, the shot, and more. I'm suggesting this because, if that's the cause, your OB/GYN will be able to help narrow it down."

"Okay. Is there anything else I should do today?"

Dr. Canton smiled. "Nope. I've sent over your information to her. She'll have what we've already ruled out and the history of migraines you reported, and so on. I'd recommend you schedule to see her as soon as possible."

At that moment, Dr. Canton's pager beeped, and she glanced at it where it sat on the counter beside her. "I need to go, my next appointment is here." As I stood, she reached out and squeezed my shoulder lightly. Her gaze shifted to Boone. "Very nice to meet you, Boone." She held out her hand, and he shook it quickly.

A few minutes later, we were walking outside, and Boone's hand was warm on my back. Once I was seated in the passenger seat, and he started the truck, I let out a big sigh. "Well, that sucks."

"It doesn't suck," he replied, his eyes wide as he glanced in my direction before backing out of the parking space. "They ruled out all the scary stuff. That's fucking awesome."

Staring at him, the tension I hadn't realized I'd been holding in a tight ball in my chest loosened and unspooled. "I guess you're right. But I wanted an answer. Something definitive."

Boone looked my way again and nodded. "I get it. Maybe you're not that relieved, but I am. In fact, I think we should get lunch to celebrate."

"Do you need to get back for work?

The steering wheel slid under his hand as he turned out of the parking space. "No. I'm not on call today. What about you?"

"I actually don't have to work tonight."

"Then, let's eat," he said with a slow smile.

A few hours later, I sat in the truck beside Boone, my body fairly humming with need. All we'd done was have lunch and run some errands afterwards. That's it.

Yet, sitting across from Boone at the deli and staring into his brown gaze had left me all hot and bothered. I'd never have thought I could stay all twisted up and needy inside for hours, but that's what happened. I was coming to discover that all it took was being near Boone to make me half lose my mind.

Chapter Eighteen

BOONE

At some point along the drive back to Stolen Hearts Valley, I glanced sideways. Grace's head was thrown back in a laugh. I wanted to freeze-frame that moment.

During the years my father had been sick, I'd learned how to compartmentalize. That ability served me well as a first responder. I could set my feelings aside, almost like putting them on a shelf to deal with when I had more emotional stamina.

I hadn't realized I'd been doing that very thing ever since I'd overheard the conversation between Grace and the receptionist, weeks ago now at the doctor's office. Although that interaction had served as the flashpoint to get me to finally stop giving

Grace space—and for that, I would be forever grateful—I hadn't even allowed myself to contemplate how much concern I was holding clenched tightly inside.

Between the vagueness of the situation and the night I saw her with that migraine, my worry would've torn me apart if I'd let myself focus on it. Instead, I had tucked it away. The relief of hearing from her doctor that all the worst options were ruled out was immense.

The drive back to Stolen Hearts Valley was reminiscent of days gone by between us. Grace wasn't holding that cold distance in front of her like a shield; we didn't have lingering worry rumbling under the surface of every moment. Instead, Grace belted out songs with me and laughed.

By the time we exited off the highway onto the winding road that led us to Stolen Hearts Valley, a light, icy cold drizzle had started to fall. Grace commented, "We need to get takeout pizza and have a fire when we get back."

"I'm in."

For an instant, I wanted to point out that it felt like old times. But I sensed that labeling it, identifying it out loud, might make Grace skittish. She was skittish by nature and even more so than she'd ever been before.

The massive misunderstanding with the way things played out between us before certainly didn't help matters, and I knew it.

"Anybody actually deliver pizza?" I asked as I turned onto the exit off the highway and came to a careful stop at the intersection.

Grace rolled her head sideways on the seat. She had kicked her shoes off, and her feet were resting on the dashboard, her striped socks barely visible in the almost darkness. "Uh-huh," she said, nodding as she lifted a hand to catch a lock of her hair and twirl it around her finger.

"Well, that's new."

"You've been here almost a year, Boone. How do you not know we can get delivery?"

I got lost for a minute staring into Grace's smoke silver eyes. When she arched a brow in question, I gave myself a mental shake. "I don't know. I usually just grab something at the deli at the grocery store."

My heart pumped hard and fast in my chest as Grace held my gaze, lifting her chin slightly. "It's rainy and cold, and I don't want to be out. Get us home, and I'll order pizza once we're there."

"Bossy much?" I teased.

She laughed. "Yes. Now drive."

Joy sent my pulse racing. Looking back toward the road, the sound of my blinker echoed in the cab of my truck during a gap between songs. It wasn't that I didn't know what I wanted. I knew exactly what I wanted.

Grace. And the chance to get it right this time.

Despite that certainty, it felt as if there was so much happening under the surface. Like this. How could it feel so meaningful to get pizza?

Grace's resistance to me had been so powerful, I felt as if I were trying to adjust the speed, shifting gears to make sure everything ran smoothly.

Once we exited off the highway, the winding roads were icy. I drove carefully, far too aware of how treacherous a rainy night on slick roads in these mountains could lead to disaster. The rain picked up, coming down in sheets, blurring my view with the windshield wipers barely able to keep pace by the time I pulled up in front of the duplex. Leaning back between the seats, I grabbed my rain jacket and handed it to Grace.

"Do you have another one?" she asked immediately when she looked over at me, her voice almost drowned out by the rain pounding on the roof of my truck.

I shook my head. "Don't worry about it. It's maybe ten steps. I can handle it."

Grace rolled her eyes, not even bothering to put the raincoat on. She lifted it over her head as she leaped out of the truck and dashed to the doorstep. I was right behind her, and we stopped under the small overhang that protected the main entrance. When I looked down to find Grace's upturned face, her eyes sparkling and her lips pink, I didn't even think.

Bending low, I caught her chin with my hand and kissed her, savoring the sweet little hitch that came from the back of her throat. Her skin was damp and cool, but her lips were warm. Angling my head to the side, I let my tongue tease against hers. For just a moment, I forgot where we were. When she flexed into me and shivered slightly, awareness broke through the haze of need and emotion clouding my thoughts, and I broke away.

After fumbling with the keys, somehow we managed to get through the door and up the stairs. Once we reached the landing, I glanced down. "Your place or mine?"

"Mine," she said with a slow smile that

never failed to elicit a hard kick of my heart. "I have to feed Wayne."

"I didn't want to assume."

Grace stilled for a moment, one hand curled on the doorknob as she looked up at me. I didn't know what thoughts passed through her mind, but after a beat, she nodded.

Once we were inside, I watched as she fussed over Wayne and got him fresh water and food. She'd handed me the rain jacket, which I shook off in the entryway. Toeing off my boots, I placed them by the door where she left her shoes.

My entire body felt tight. Need had its claws deep in me, and timing had nothing to say about this. I felt as if the guardrails I'd tried so valiantly to hold in place had fallen, and we were careening off the tracks.

Grace turned, her eyes catching mine as I walked toward where she stood by the kitchen window. The air felt electric—loaded and heavy—the way it felt when thunder was rumbling and lightning was about to strike. The rain poured down outside, a cacophony of raindrops striking the roof.

She took several steps in my direction as I closed the distance between us. We stopped, maybe a foot between us, beside the small island that separated the living room from the kitchen.

I almost didn't trust myself. My hands were practically shaking from the restraint of snatching her to me and devouring every inch of her.

Grace made the first move, lifting her hand and placing her palm over my heart. It kicked against my ribs, almost as if it actually knew who she was. On an elemental level, every cell in my body was attuned to Grace.

"Boone..." she began before pausing and biting her lip.

I placed my hand over hers and took a step closer. "What?"

"I need you."

Her words fell into the quiet, providing kindling for the fire burning between us. It felt as if little bolts of lightning were striking and electrifying the air around us.

"You have me."

Then, our lips collided. We were swept into the roaring current of lust, desire, and pure want. I was barely aware of anything beyond Grace and the feel of her body in my arms. In a tangle of lips, teeth, and tongue, we tore at each other's clothes.

It was awkward and inefficient because I didn't want to stop kissing her. Her shirt got caught in her hair. She had my fly undone and started shoving my jeans around my hips before I interrupted her again to cup her face and fit my mouth over hers. Somehow, I managed to get her down to her panties with her blouse partially unbuttoned.

Her palm slid into my boxers, curling over my cock, which was hard as steel. My mouth broke from hers on a ragged groan. "Fuck, Grace."

She giggled, her lips pressing hot kisses along my jawline and sending streaks of fire under the surface of my skin. Yanking at her blouse, I barely registered the sound of a button pinging on the hardwood floor. All I knew was a sense of sheer relief when the fabric fell open, and I could finally dip my head to swirl my tongue around one of her nipples. It puckered tightly through the lace as I bit down gently, cupping her other breast while squeezing her nipple between my thumb and forefinger.

Grace gasped, a ragged moan escaping as I turned her and pressed her hips against the counter. I lifted my head just long enough to flick my thumb on the clasp of her bra between her breasts, letting out a satisfied growl as her plump breasts tumbled free, the two lacy cups falling to her sides. Her dusky pink nipples were tight, and I didn't even bother to wait. I immediately leaned down again and swirled my tongue around one, savoring the sweet tang of her skin and the feel of her fingers spearing into my hair and stinging my scalp as she held on.

Reaching around between her supple thighs, I cupped my palm over her mound, my fingers teasing over the damp cotton. "Boone!" she gasped. "Don't wait. I need you. Now." She turned toward me again, her words husky and demanding.

With a light nip on her neck, I lifted my head. "Bossy, aren't we?"

Her eyes flashed as her hips bucked slightly. "Yes. Now." She ordered as she reached to where my fly hung open, shoving my boxers out of the way and freeing my cock. When her hand curled around me and slid up the hard length in a firm stroke, I quickly saw her point.

Spinning her around, I ordered, "Bend over."

Grace, not usually one to follow orders, complied immediately. When she leaned her elbows on the tile counter, the sweet curve in her spine and the tilt of her bottom sent a jolt of blood straight to my already aching cock. With one hand, I yanked her panties down, and she kicked them free from her ankles. At the sight of her pink, glistening pussy, a low growl escaped. Sliding my hand over the lush curve of her ass, I let my fingers tease in her soaking wet folds.

"Mmm, so wet," I murmured as I sank two fingers inside of her.

Grace's head fell forward between her elbows as she let out a little cry, her hips pressing back into my touch. I stroked my cock with my free hand, pre-cum beading on the tip and rolling down while I clung to my control.

"Boone," she gasped as I stroked my fingers inside of her once again, "I said now."

"Yes ma'am." Sliding my fingers free, I nudged the crown of my cock against her entrance, holding still for just a beat before surging inside in a single deep thrust.

Her core gripped around me, a slick, velvety sheath. "Ahhh, Grace," I murmured as I gripped her hip with one hand and slid my palm up her back to lace my fingers in her hair. "You make me crazy."

Her reply was incoherent as she rocked back into me. I drew back once, sliding in slow and deep before I lost control and powered into her with deep, pounding strokes. Her hands curled over the edge of the counter in front of her as her hips arched to meet me.

Everything was a blur of driving, pounding need. Grace cried out, her body tightening as I released her hair. I reached around to tease my fingers over her swollen clit, savoring the feel of her channel throbbing around me and clamping down tightly when my name came in a rough shout as she found her release.

My own release came thundering on the heels of hers as if a bolt of lightning struck my body, and every cell went taut. The pressure was almost unbearable before it snapped loose and whipsawed through me as I poured my release into her. I dropped kisses up her spine as I pushed her blouse up to her shoulders, savoring the little shivers of her body and the tremors around me.

When I pressed a kiss to the back of her neck, Grace let out a soft sigh. My heart clenched. There'd been a time when I didn't think I would ever have this with Grace again. At that moment, I heard her stomach growl, and she giggled, the sound spinning through me.

"We forgot to order pizza," I murmured against her skin.

Chapter Nineteen

GRACE

I wanted to stay exactly where I was. With Boone curled around me, stretching and filling me even as he went soft. I giggled again when my stomach growled. "I suppose we did forget about the pizza."

Boone pressed a soft, open-mouthed kiss right at the sensitive spot behind my ear, sending goosebumps rising in the wake of his touch. Much to my disappointment, he lifted his head, tugging my blouse down as he withdrew from me. He turned me around, stepping close to give me a lingering kiss. When our eyes collided, I felt caught in the power of his gaze.

Boone had always had this way about him, when his eyes held mine, his gaze was sexy and loving all at once. He made me feel as if I were the very center of his universe. Once upon a time, I had no fear from the intensity of that feeling. Yet, I'd since learned just how much it hurt to lose that, and I didn't want to let my guard down too easily again.

Shaking those thoughts away, I forced my eyes from his, surveying the disarray around us. His T-shirt had been thrown on the floor at some point while my jeans were half-hanging off the edge of the couch nearby, and my panties were a bright cotton purple splotch on the tile beside the cabinets.

"We're going to have to get dressed before the pizza guy shows up," I said as I finally braved another look at him.

"Oh, for sure," he replied, his lips kicking up in a smile.

I shimmied out from between him and the counter, quickly walking over to snag my panties and jeans and tug them on. Whether he sensed my internal distress or not, Boone followed my lead, tucking himself back into his jeans and putting his shirt on.

Once he was dressed, he pulled out his phone and glanced over. "Tell me where to call in an order. Pepperoni still your favorite?"

My heart gave a hop, skip, and a jump at the realization that he remembered that detail about me. I was in *so* much trouble. I was on the verge of tears over learning Boone remembered pepperoni was my favorite kind of pizza. It was only a little bit ridiculous. Okay, maybe a lot.

Swallowing through the emotion slamming into me, I nodded. "Of course," I replied, striving to keep my tone light. "Call Lost Deer. They do pizza delivery from the restaurant," I said, quickly reciting their number.

Not much later, with the rain still drumming on the roof, Boone and I were sitting on the couch with my legs draped over his lap and the pizza box sitting on my thighs while we ate straight out of the box. Wayne sat on the opposite side of Boone, resuming the allegiance he'd once had to him. It felt as if the clock had spun backwards and plunged us into another time and place along the continuum.

Doubts kept feathering along the edges of my thoughts. But honestly, it felt too good to let myself dwell in that place of worry.

"Oh my God, dumb decision," Boone murmured, his eyes on the television screen as a couple made a choice about a house purchase.

"Why is it a dumb decision?"

He lifted another piece of pizza, his gaze sliding to mine. "Because it's one of those old houses. Just replacing the boiler alone is going to cost them a small fortune. Don't get me wrong, I love those old houses, but you need to be willing to do the work yourself, or you have to be independently wealthy. That couple is neither."

I laughed as I leaned forward and bit off the end of the slice of pizza he held in his hands. The two pieces of pepperoni were too perfectly placed for me to resist.

"Hey," he said, pulling the piece out of my reach. "I think this is mine."

Grinning, I shrugged. "It was right there."

He held my gaze for a beat, and my pulse kicked up a notch. Leaning over, he pressed a lingering kiss on the side of my neck, sending my belly into flips and heat blooming through me.

"I always loved that you loved pizza," he murmured as he drew away and took a bite of his pizza.

"Yeah?" My pulse galloped along, and I picked up another piece of pizza.

"Yeah," he said gruffly. "I loved a lot of things about you, Grace. I never stopped."

When I looked over, my eyes snagged on his, and my heartbeat stuttered before lunging forcefully again.

———

"Sirloin tips! Rare," one of the line cooks called as I burst through the swinging door at the restaurant.

I had a tray full of dirty dishes propped on my shoulder and hurried back toward the dishwasher area. Lowering the tray onto the stainless steel table beside the industrial dishwasher, I cast a quick smile at the newest hire. He was a teenager still in high school named Bradley. "Thanks, Bradley."

I felt my ponytail swing as I turned and raced toward the pick-up counter across from the line cooks, who were moving at lightning speed. "Anything else with the sirloin tips yet?" I asked as I glanced across.

One of the guys nodded. "I've got the rainbow trout ready right here." He deftly turned and slid it out of the oven, putting the trout on a plate and adding a garnish of kale and lemon.

"Thanks, guys," I called over my shoulder

as I grabbed a clean tray from the rack and situated more plates on it.

The evening flew by. I was relieved to be so busy because I was feeling so rattled inside by Boone and what was unfolding between us. He'd spent the night with me after our pizza and intense encounter in the kitchen.

Because it was us, the chemistry just wouldn't quit. I'd woken during the night with him curled up behind me, the hard, velvet length of his cock nestled against my bottom. When I'd shifted my hips, he'd pressed a soft kiss against the back of my neck.

"Hey, baby." His whispered greeting had made me bite my lip.

"How long have you been awake?" I'd asked in the darkness.

"You woke me up."

Kiss.

"I don't think so." Reaching between us, I nudged my hips suggestively against his arousal, feeling the slick heat between my thighs.

"Baby, I don't have to be awake to want you."

Then, his hands mapped my body, skillfully teasing between my thighs. Somehow he got my panties off and lifted my thigh. His cock slid between my folds, my juices making him slide easily back and forth. The crown of his cock rubbing over my clit had nearly driven me mad.

"Boone," I pleaded. "You're teasing me."

"I want to go slow." The feel of his lips moving against that sensitive skin right where my shoulder joined my neck had me arching and letting out a soft cry when he rocked again.

"I don't want you to go slow."

"Okay. Whatever you want."

Then, I felt the sweet, delicious slide of him inside me, the fit tight and the stretch intoxicating.

We found our release together with him nudging inside of me as I rocked against him. My climax came slow and deep, shattering me inside and out.

"Grace?"

Evie's voice broke through the haze of recollection. I realized I was just standing there by the station where we refilled salt and pepper shakers and so on.

Giving my head an actual shake, I turned to look at her. "Hey. What's up?"

"Hey, yourself. You're kind of zoning out. You're not getting another headache, are you?"

"Oh, no. I swear, I'm not."

"Okay. There's one last table to serve. Dani's closed up the front. Want to go to Lost Deer after we're done?" she asked, referring to pretty much the only place we hung out after hours other than here at the lodge restaurant.

For a split second, I hesitated, wondering if Boone would be home. That hesitation galvanized me to say yes. I did *not* need to be letting him change the course of my social life.

"Sure. I'm guessing more people are going."

"Of course. Shay and Jackson'll be there and some of the guys from the crew. Maybe even Boone," Evie teased, a gleam in her bright blue eyes.

My cheeks heated as I rolled my eyes. "Maybe so. Who's up for the last table?"

"Well, if you'd been paying attention, you'd know it was you," she said with a pointed look. "But, I'll take it."

"I got it," I said, nudging her with my elbow and hurrying back out front.

Chapter Twenty

BOONE

I leaned my elbow against the table as I lifted my beer to take a long drag, setting it down with a sigh. "Damn, that's some good beer."

Walker, usually rather quiet, nodded firmly. "Damn straight. There are so many breweries," he began, using air quotes with his fingers around breweries, "that you never know which ones are actually any good. This place is good."

"I even like their wine," Dawson offered with a slow grin.

"Agreed. I had some of their wine at the fundraiser they did for the rescue program a few months back. All they served was wine. I guess they think rich people only drink wine," I commented.

Jackson threw his head back with a laugh. "I wouldn't know. I didn't decide on the drink menu."

"Me neither," his girlfriend, Shay, chimed in. "When they offered us the space at no charge, we just went for it."

My phone vibrated in my pocket, and I slipped it out to see a voice mail banner. My mother had called twice today, but I hadn't had time to call her back, nor had time to even listen to her messages. I made a mental note to call her on my way home.

After a busy day of training, including helping the local firefighter crew handle a practice burn, most of the crew headed to Lost Deer Bar for burgers and beer. I was hoping with Shay there that I might luck out and see Grace. Just then, I decided the stars were shining down on me when I heard her voice.

Looking over my shoulder, I saw her approaching our table with Evie. Evie was one of Grace's closest friends from high school. When it came to friends, it had been a tad awkward for me when I first moved back. Our social worlds overlapped, and it appeared most of the women were aligned with Grace even though not a one of them knew the details of what had happened.

Dawson stood to greet Evie. "Hey, girl," he said, pulling her close to his side. He dropped a lingering kiss on her lips.

I looked away, wishing Grace and I were in a place where I could be that open with her. She stopped right beside my chair, and I glanced at her. "Have a seat." I nudged my chin toward the seat beside me, almost letting out a sigh of relief when she sat down.

"Want a drink?" I asked.

Her teeth sank into her bottom lip, her cheeks tinged with pink as her lashes fell, brushing against her cheeks before she opened them again. "I'll take some wine. You don't have to get it for me," she said as I lifted my hand to catch the attention of our waitress who was delivering drinks at a table nearby.

Looking back at Grace, I said, "Either let me get a drink for you, or give me a kiss."

Grace's cheeks flushed a deeper shade of pink as her eyes shifted to scan the table. She murmured, "Okay, you can get me a drink." There was a hint of warning in her tone.

"Are we a secret then?" I asked, knowing I was pushing my luck here.

The waitress arrived, stopping beside me. "What can I get for you?"

"She'll take a glass of wine. What kind?" I looked at Grace.

"Just the house red, please."

"Got it." The waitress stepped past us, immediately checking in with the rest of the new arrivals, including Evie, Valentina, and Lucas.

"Well?" I asked as I leaned my other elbow on the table and angled my head to the side. Her hair was in a messy ponytail, and she had her glasses on, which I fucking loved.

"I don't know," she finally said. "Do we have to have this conversation now?"

I relented and shrugged, just so happy Grace wasn't treating me like I didn't even exist. Our group settled into an easy banter, and I almost thanked Lucas when he snagged an extra chair so he could sit down with us, creating the need for Grace to scoot her chair even closer to mine.

When I slid my hand on her thigh and she didn't swat it away, I took that for the win that it was. Evie caught my eyes and gave me a small smile. Although she hadn't said a word to me about Grace, I sensed she might be rooting for me.

Grace sipped her wine, picking up the thread of a conversation interrupted several times now. "Didn't you say Mack was moving back?" she asked Evie, referring to Evie's older brother.

Evie nodded. "So he says. Although he said the same thing last fall."

"Sure be good to see him," I commented. Mack and I had been friends in high school. We stayed in touch sporadically, and he was one of the few who knew just how badly things had skidded sideways for me. He'd been traveling out in Colorado and visited with me during the months after everything went to shit for me with Grace.

Evie cast a quick smile in my direction. "I know. He loves to travel, but it'd be nice to get to see more of him."

"Any idea when he might come back?" Jackson asked. "One of the guys on our crew is moving away, so he'd have a guaranteed job if he doesn't miss the chance."

"I wish he'd say when, but I'll make sure to tell him to call you. Maybe that'll push him to make a decision," Evie replied.

"He sounds as vague as Ash is about moving home," Shay commented, referring to Jackson's younger sister. I honestly didn't know where she was.

"Maybe we should ask Mack to bring Ash with him when he moves back," Jackson teased.

I felt Grace shift slightly and glanced her way reflexively. I couldn't help myself and leaned over. "What are the chances I can see you later?"

When she bit her lip and smiled, I wanted to pound my chest in celebration. Just as I thought that maybe, just maybe, Grace and I might be headed in a good direction, it all went to hell.

"Boone," a voice said, an unfortunately familiar voice.

I turned to glance over my shoulder, incredulous. Diana approached the table. I felt the moment Grace turned to look as well. *Oh hell* didn't even capture the clusterfuck this could become.

Diana held absolutely zero appeal for me. Yet, I could objectively see what drew me to her the one single night that had blown up so much of my life. She was tall with generous curves and gave off a classic beachy vibe with her sun-kissed dark blond hair and blue eyes.

She stopped at the table, looking down at me. "Hi, Boone," she said casually with a bright smile. Despite her smile, she had a brittle quality to her, and I didn't know what that was about.

"What the hell are you doing here, Diana?" I blurted out.

The smile was wiped off of Diana's face instantly. To say we hadn't been on good terms after I found out the way she misled me was an understatement. Her face tightened and pain flashed in her eyes. A pain I didn't really care to process with her.

"I was hoping we could talk," she said.

Grace had tensed beside me, quickly shifting her legs away and leaving me no choice but for my hand to fall off of her without making a show of it. I took a slow breath, trying to quell my irritation.

A quick glance around the table, and it was obvious to me that we had a true audience by this point. The conversation that had been murmuring around us quieted, and all eyes were on Diana.

With zero good options for dealing with this situation, I did the only thing I could think to do. Standing, I said, "I don't know why you're here, but I guess we should go outside and talk."

I didn't wait to see if Diana followed me. I strode quickly across the bar and out the back door, frustration simmering inside. Once I stepped outside, I turned. Diana curled her arms around her waist and said, "Boone, you don't have to be that rude to me."

"For fuck's sake, Diana. How the hell did you find me here?"

"Luck really. I tried calling your mother, but she wouldn't tell me a thing."

So that's what my mom had probably called about. I definitely needed to thank her for trying to keep Diana out of my orbit.

"I knew you moved here because you talked about this place before you stopped talking to me." Diana paused, as if I might offer something up. I didn't. "Anyway, maybe it's crazy, but I hoped we could talk, so I flew out here. I saw your truck outside when I was driving by and hoped it was the right one."

Although Diana and I didn't get involved after our single night together, during her months-long lie, she saw me more than a few times. I still drove the same damn truck and was silently cursing myself for not bothering to get a new one.

"Look, Diana, you lied to me about something major. Like I said before, I know what happened was difficult for you, just like it was for me. But we're not going to be friends. I have no fucking clue why you're here."

Diana burst into tears.

Fuck my life.

A cold gust of air blew across the parking

lot. Feeling hemmed in by my lack of options, I gestured for her to follow me to my truck. I figured we might as well talk there. Once we were both inside, I started the truck for the sole purpose of running the heat. It was almost spring, but the mountain nights were still cool.

Diana opened her purse and pulled out a small packet of tissues. After dabbing at her eyes and blowing her nose, she glanced over to me. "I know I screwed up, Boone. But you went through it with me, and I don't know who else to talk to. I'm not doing so well."

My mouth must've actually dropped open as I stared at her.

"Don't look at me like that. We lost a baby."

"It wasn't *our* baby. You led me to believe it was, and I went through hell over it. You lied and totally fucked with me. If your mother hadn't told me the truth later on, I probably still wouldn't know it. That's on you. I *am* sorry for what you're going through, but this isn't something I can help you with."

Diana stared at me for a long moment. She surprised me by nodding. "I know. I owe you an apology, and I wanted to tell you face to face. I really am sorry. I guess it's been on my mind because, well, I just had another miscarriage. For some crazy reason, it made me want to talk to you."

When she lifted her hands and let them fall, I shook my head slowly. I felt for her. I really did, but I couldn't do this. I just couldn't.

Chapter Twenty-One

GRACE

Humiliation was a cold, heavy weight in my chest. This awful feeling was precisely what I had tried to avoid back when Boone basically fell off the face of the earth to me. Here I sat with all of our mutual friends, and he had just walked out with some gorgeous woman who showed up out of nowhere.

There was a moment of stunned silence, and then everyone tried to make an effort to smooth it over. The waitress conveniently arrived to deliver some appetizers someone had ordered, and small talk rose in murmurs around me.

Evie caught my eyes from across the table, her gaze concerned. I looked away. I didn't know what the hell was going on or what to do. I felt bereft. When there was enough of a murmur going on, I took that moment to excuse myself. "I'm gonna head out for the night. I've got an early shift in the morning as it is."

Evie caught me by the elbow as I walked down the hallway to go to the bathroom before I left. "Hey, are you okay?"

Turning, I met her eyes and shrugged. "Sure. Some gorgeous girl showed up out of nowhere, and Boone left to talk to her. I'm totally fine."

"Don't go to the worst possible scenario," Evie said quickly. "I'm sure Boone can explain."

"Maybe. It doesn't really matter right now. I'm going home."

"Call me?"

"About what?" I countered, honestly curious.

"As soon as you get a chance to talk to Boone, let me know if you're okay."

I bit back a sigh. "Sure. See you tomorrow."

When I stepped out into the chilly darkness, I tugged my jacket around me as I hurried across the parking lot. I cursed myself for even noticing Boone's truck. It was running, and I could see the silhouette of two people inside. I tore my eyes away.

With my gut churning, I drove home quickly, letting myself into my quiet apartment and making sure to bolt the door on the landing upstairs.

When there was a knock on my door over an hour later, I ignored it. My heart just felt tired.

"Grace," Boone's voice called through the door. "Please let me explain."

Although Boone only knocked a few times, I still hardly slept. Restless at around two a.m., I rolled out of bed, made myself a pot of coffee, sat down on the couch with Wayne beside me, and got to work on my dissertation. When all else failed, at least I could mostly distract myself by burying my thoughts in academics.

Three hours later, I climbed in the shower and left the house early. Luck was on my side, at least for this morning. His truck was already gone. I didn't even let myself think about why that might be. When I got to the restaurant, Dani's brows hitched up high when she saw me coming in through the back door.

Dani had likely already been there for an hour. She had a streak of flour on her cheek, and her apron was dusted with cinnamon and flour. I guessed on the cinnamon because that was what she smelled like when I paused beside her.

"Mornin'. Should I make a fresh pot of coffee?" I asked, striving to keep my tone casual and hoping my lack of sleep wasn't apparent.

Dani's gaze searched my face before she nodded. "I'd love a fresh pot of coffee. Jackson and a few of the guys from the crew came by for coffee about an hour ago. They had an early call."

Instantly, my gut tightened as I wondered if Boone happened to be with them. When I walked over to the counter that ran along the wall parallel to the table where Dani was working, she answered my unspoken question.

"Boone was here. He looked like hell. Did you talk to him last night?"

Scooping coffee into the filter, I paused to glance over my shoulder. "No, I didn't talk to him. Last I saw, he was busy talking to Diana."

I shoved the coffee filter in the basket and hit the start button before I turned back. I rested my hips against the counter, crossing my arms tightly.

Dani resumed what I guessed she'd been working on before I came in, carefully slicing strips of rolled dough and spooning filling in them before rolling them into tidy pinwheels. I sensed she was giving me a moment or so to stew. My guess was right when she spoke. "Are you done being pissed off now?"

"Maybe," I replied, my tone dry.

Dani chuckled. "Fine. Well, I'll tell you what Boone told me this morning. The only reason he walked out to talk to her was to avoid a scene in the middle of the bar. I'm sure you can agree with that."

When Dani arched a brow and eyed me, I nodded. "Yes," I replied tersely.

"Anyway, it was his ex—" She paused, then shook her head. "Actually, I don't want to call her his ex. It was a one-night stand when he was twenty. They never actually dated. You know that, right?"

"That's what he told me. I'm starting to get the idea you know more about this than I do." I couldn't help the mulish tone in my voice.

"I doubt it. Boone told me he knocked on your door last night, and you wouldn't answer. As for the rest of the story, he told Wade about it not too long ago, and his mother told my mother about it. That's it.

I'm sure you can agree that what Diana did was a total mindfuck for him."

I nodded. "We can definitely agree on that."

It took all I had not to ask her what else Boone had told her this morning. Because Dani was more gracious than I was feeling this morning, she offered it up without me asking. "Long story short, I guess she got pregnant *again* by the same asshole from before. The very guy she decided not to tell about her first pregnancy because she thought Boone was a better candidate for a father." Dani rolled her eyes, hard, at that.

"She got pregnant again and came to talk to Boone about it?" I couldn't even hide the complete shock in my tone.

Dani nodded. "That's not the whole story though. She had another miscarriage, and I guess she's a fucking train wreck. Lord knows why she wanted to come talk to Boone, but people don't always act rationally." Dani paused in her work to shrug. "He said after she burst out into tears, she said some stuff about how she needed to come to apologize in person finally. I told him it's obvious she was probably feeling him out to see if there was a chance for them."

Staring at Dani, I took a slow breath, letting it out with a gusty sigh. "What the hell? I feel bad for her. I mean, I can't imagine going through two miscarriages. But what is she thinking? After lying to Boone like that, how could she think he'd want anything to do with her?"

Dani's lips set in a thin line. She closed her eyes briefly, but not before I saw the pain flash in their depths. Dani had a miscarriage when she was younger, and it had almost killed her. Although the circumstances were different, the reverberating effects of that event in her life had caused her a lot of pain.

When she opened her eyes again, she nodded. "Obviously, it's awful. I don't think she's thinking clearly. Boone made sure she was set up in a hotel last night, but he has no idea what to do. I suggested he call her family. I don't know her, but it doesn't sound like she can rely on that other guy for any emotional support."

The coffee maker beeped behind me. Relieved for the distraction, I turned and snagged two mugs from the shelf above it. I filled them both and carried them over to where Dani was working. "Did you want cream?"

Dani shrugged. "I'll take it black. The mood calls for it."

Glancing at the clock above the door that led into the restaurant kitchen, I saw that I had enough time to enjoy this coffee with her before I started work. Slipping my hips on the stool across from her, I took a long swallow, contemplating what she'd just shared with me.

"What a mess," I said after a few sips of coffee.

"You're telling me." Dani paused as she finished rolling another pastry and set it on the tray. After a sip of her coffee, she asked, "Are you going to talk to Boone, or start ignoring him again?"

Twisting a lock of hair around my finger, I nodded. "Yes. It's just...I'm not sure what's best right now. Boone has a tendency to make me forget my concerns. Trust is kind of an issue for me. That's not just because of Boone."

"I know. Guys can be real assholes. John was no help with trust," she said.

"I know," I replied. Sometimes I just wanted to throw in the towel when it came to romance.

Dani continued, "I honestly think Boone really wants this to work. I'm pretty sure he was desperate when he talked to me this morning. They came in for an early training exercise but then got a call. If I get an update from Wade, I'll let you know."

"What's the call for?"

Considering that I had several friends on the first responder team, I was accustomed to having people I cared about doing risky things. Yet, the stakes felt so much higher with Boone.

"An accident in an area where they were repairing a bridge. One of the workers fell into the ravine. I'm sure it'll be fine. At least, that's what I tell myself every single time Wade goes out on a call."

I sighed. "I bet you do."

Chapter Twenty-Two

BOONE

After a long day, I returned home, hoping like hell that Grace was there. My arms were aching. Every muscle in my body was throbbing. A guy doing construction work on a bridge over a ravine had fallen and gotten trapped below. Jackson, Lucas, and I had worked together to get him safely out of there. We'd spent hours in our climbing gear, hanging onto cold, wet rocks and branches to get it done.

When Grace's car wasn't there when I drove up, I simply walked straight into my shower. I stood under the steaming water for far longer than I probably needed. I felt half human after my shower and downing several ibuprofen. When I peeked out the front window and saw Grace's car, I decided not to wait.

Jogging down the stairs, I ignored my aching muscles as I rounded the entryway at the bottom and promptly climbed up the stairs on the opposite side. I understood she'd been pissed off enough last night to make sure I couldn't walk through the door on the upper landing. But damn, I wouldn't have minded it today.

I didn't realize I was holding my breath after I knocked until Grace opened the door. My breath released, tension unspooling at the sight of her. Her hair was pulled up in a messy ponytail with one lock falling loose. Her purple streaks had faded to a soft lavender. Her silver-gray gaze met mine, and we simply stared at each other for a moment. Just then, I realized I hadn't even bothered to fully dress when her eyes flicked down to my bare feet. I had yanked on a pair of jeans and a T-shirt and nothing else before hurrying over here.

"Can I come in?"

"Of course." She stepped back, letting the door swing open.

The moment I stepped inside, Wayne leaped off the windowsill and trotted across the room to twine around my ankles. Leaning down, I scratched between his ears as Grace laughed softly.

Closing the door behind us, she commented, "He's almost blind, but he knows it's you."

Straightening, I shrugged. "I wish you were as happy to see me."

Grace's mouth twisted as her eyes flicked away before returning to mine. "Dani explained what happened."

"Oh," I said, surprised. I had unloaded on Dani this morning, primarily out of stress after a sleepless night. Also, because I honestly didn't know what the hell to do about Diana.

"The rescue went okay?" Grace asked.

"Oh yeah. I'm just tired." My stomach let out an audible growl at that moment.

She gestured for me to follow her over to the kitchen. "Have a seat. I'll make you something to eat. Or, would you rather get pizza?"

Slipping my hips onto the stool she pulled out for me, I shrugged. "Totally your call. I'll eat anything, and you're a good cook."

Grace smiled. "Let me see what I've got." As she rummaged in the refrigerator, I leaned my elbows on the counter as the weariness set in. Fuck, I was exhausted.

"I've got a pan of Dani's lasagna in the freezer. I can have it ready in about twenty minutes," Grace called over her shoulder.

"Sounds perfect."

While she pulled out the lasagna and turned on the oven, she continued talking, "I'll make some garlic bread to go with it too."

When she looked over, and I saw anxiety flickering in her eyes, my heart squeezed. "You don't have to cook for me, Grace. I'm guessing you might be pissed off about last night."

"I was, but I'm not now. I swear. Have you talked to Diana since last night?"

I'd already decided brutal honesty was the only way to go. "I called her on the drive home after I called her mother. We're not close. At all. But I figured her family should know where she was. Grace, I don't know what to say. I feel bad for her, but I really can't be there for her."

Grace had pulled out a loaf of bread, and I immediately recognized the label—fresh bread from Wake & Bake Café, a popular local place in town. My mouth started watering, but I kept my focus on the conversation. She started slicing the bread and put butter in a pan to melt with crushed garlic.

"I'm angry about what she did to you, but I feel terrible she's going through this again. Is she going to fly back home?"

"Yeah. Her mom already bought her a ticket. I think she's pretty embarrassed. Lord knows why she hooked up with that guy again. He doesn't seem like the nicest guy. With that and her having another miscarriage, well, I can't even imagine how she's feeling."

Grace stirred the melting butter as she looked over at me. After a beat, she offered, "I certainly don't hold it against her for not having great judgment around men. I haven't exactly been a winner in that area."

I literally felt the barb of those words as a visceral sting on the surface of my heart, almost flinching. Grace must've seen the expression on my face because her eyes widened.

"I wasn't talking about you. Since we're being honest, there's only one other guy I kind of got serious with. I say 'kind of' because it was a one-way street. He cheated on me with a girl in my grad program."

Anger jolted through me, hot and furious. "Fucking asshole," I said flatly. "Can you tell me who he is so I can kick his ass?"

Her smile was bitter. "Leave it alone,

Boone. It's just I didn't see it coming, you know? Anyway, I'm mad at Diana for what she did to you, but I feel really bad for her."

"Yeah, me too. That whole situation with her was just nuts." I paused, uncertain what else to say.

Grace turned off the burner and lifted the pot, slowly pouring it over the loaf of sliced bread. "Damn, that looks good, sugar."

The endearment just slipped out. We'd gotten comfortable enough these last few weeks. My eyes swung to hers. Grace met my gaze, holding it as her lips curled into a small smile.

"I'm glad you're here, Boone," she said softly.

Emotion hit me so hard, my chest tightened. "You have no idea how much that means."

I hadn't realized how afraid I was that she'd shut me out again until she didn't. I stood, ignoring my protesting muscles and walked around the island to step behind her and slide my arms around her waist. Dipping my chin into the sweet curve of her neck, I dropped a soft kiss there.

"You're distracting me," she murmured.

"Don't worry, this is about all I can do."

Leaning back, she turned her head to the side and looked at me. "Are you okay?"

"Just sore. We had to do a lot of climbing today. I just need the ibuprofen to kick in." My stomach growled loudly. "And I could seriously use some food."

Grace pressed a kiss to my cheek and nudged me back. "Go sit down on the couch with Wayne. The food will be ready in a few minutes, and you need to rest."

Much as I didn't want to leave the warmth of her body, I was too damn tired to do much else other than sit down. "Following orders," I teased as I stepped back, letting my arms fall away from her.

I must've dozed off for a few minutes, but the scent of the garlic bread woke me up. I opened my eyes to see Grace quietly setting a plate with the sliced bread on the coffee table by the couch. Her eyes whipped up to mine. "Oh! I was trying to be quiet."

"I need to eat more than I need to sleep."

She hurried back to the kitchen. "The lasagna's ready too. Don't move, I'm bringing it over. What do you want to drink?" she called.

"I'll take some water. I need to hydrate."

I propped myself up with an extra cushion behind my back as I leaned forward to snag several slices of the garlic bread. When I bit into it, the rich, buttery, garlic flavor elicited a moan of satisfaction. "Fuck, this is so good, Grace," I said as she returned with the pan of lasagna and two bowls.

She set the lasagna down on an oven mitt on the coffee table and shooed Wayne away when he sniffed at it. "You can't eat that." She gave him a stern look.

"Amazing," I said for emphasis when I took another bite of the bread.

She looked up from serving lasagna in one of the bowls. "It's just garlic bread, Boone."

"Yeah, but it's incredible."

The last thing I remembered that night was collapsing against the pillows after eating and telling Grace she'd better not let me fall asleep alone on the couch. I came awake to the feel of her lips dusting my cheek. I was in her bed with the sheets tangled around my legs and her smelling like fresh soap.

"Where are you going?" I asked as I dragged my eyes open.

"I'm working a shift this morning. Sleep as late as you need. I unlocked the door upstairs again."

"You work too much." I tried to coax her onto the bed with a little tug on her waist.

"I need the tips, and I'm going to be late."

She smiled as she pressed another quick kiss to my forehead and stood quickly. My body was still tired, and I couldn't bring myself to get up. "I'll see you later." She hurried out of the room, and I fell back asleep almost instantly.

GRACE

Dr. Sue, my OB-GYN, looked up from her computer tablet. "I probably could've saved you a bit of trouble if you'd come to me as soon as you got the migraines. Based on this timeline, you started getting them about two months after I started you on that new birth control pill."

I let out a sigh. "Fine. I should've checked with you. I just didn't connect the headaches to my birth control. Plus, that's the one that you recommended."

"True, and it works for many women. But side effects happen. There are plenty of options. We can try a different pill, or you can switch to an IUD or the shot. Your call."

"Are you sure it's the pill?"

She set her computer tablet on the counter before looking back in my direction. "We're not sure. But the quickest way to find out is to switch it. Within a month or so, we should know."

"And if it's not that?"

"Then, you're one of those unlucky people who get migraines for no specific medical reason. It's not the end of the world, although I do understand it's miserable. So, let's discuss your options. I want you to stop taking that pill immediately."

"I can stop just like that?"

"According to your prescription, as of yesterday, you just finished the last cycle. So your timing for this appointment couldn't have been better."

"Now, let's get down to the nitty-gritty. The last time we discussed your birth control, you were not in a committed relationship, but you wanted to stay on birth control for consistency. Is that still the case?" she asked matter-of-factly.

The last time I'd actually discussed my sex life with my doctor had been when I was dating John. She caught my eye, and I sighed. "Well, I'm no longer with that asshole who turned out to be cheating on me."

"Are you sexually active though? I'm not asking to be nosy."

"You asked that like you're asking what I had for breakfast."

Dr. Sue smiled slightly. "To me, it's as basic as breakfast. Because of your irregular periods before, I would recommend something to manage that. If you're sexually active, I'd recommend also using condoms to protect from STD's."

I certainly didn't want to get into my internal indecision around Boone. "I am sexually active and only with one person." There. At least I told the truth.

After she ran through the options, I settled on a hormonal IUD because it had the least side effects. She had me take ibuprofen because she warned me I would experience some cramping after the insertion. I scheduled a followup appointment six weeks later because she wanted enough time to see how I did with the change.

After I left her office, I drove into Asheville. I had a meeting with my dissertation advisor and didn't want to do it over the phone. My mind kept bouncing around on Boone. Given the circumstances, I didn't think I overreacted to Diana's appearance, but it had gotten me thinking. Just like I had before, I was letting things roll along too quickly as far as the state of my heart.

After Boone and I broke up before, I hadn't dated anyone for a bit, and then I'd frantically tried to find someone to love. The frantic quality of my feelings had been two-fold. There'd been my bruised pride and the underlying insecurity that so many women fell prey to in our world. No matter what we told ourselves, society bombarded us with messages about how we needed to find a man. Even worse, we're supposed to find a man, but also be independent and brilliant. The social standards we faced were enough to make us crazy.

So yeah, I made some not-so-great choices when it came to men after Boone and now had plenty of trust issues to lug around.

My doctor's question about whether I was exclusive with anyone was quite pre-scient. I didn't have the answer. My heart— my not-so-smart heart that wanted old wounds to heal over once and for all—was driving this boat blindly.

Walking down the hallway to my advisor's office, I heard someone say my name as I rounded the corner. I recognized the voice, all too well. As if conjured by the circum-stances in my life, John, my asshole ex was walking down the hall, a smile on his face. Fuck my life.

He stopped in front of me, leaning his shoulder against the wall. "Hey, Grace. I thought that was you."

I smiled tightly. "Hi, John. As you can see it is, in fact, me." I moved to step around him, but his hand caught me at the elbow. Looking back, I asked, "What?"

"I think an apology is overdue."

"I'm not looking for your apology, John. We've been over for a long time."

"Better late than never, right?" He threw one of his roguish smiles in my direction. With his shaggy brown hair, blue eyes, and classically handsome features, John had once charmed me far too easily.

However, it didn't work this time. I observed his effect from a detached point of view. That little twinkle in his blue eyes, the teasing smile, and the way he held my gaze as if I were the only woman in the world.

Right. For John, there was never just any one woman in the world. After I had found out about him cheating on me with another woman in my graduate program, I later found out that wasn't the first. I was well over it. Well, except for that pesky trust problem.

"Sure, if you need to apologize, go ahead."

I gave my elbow a little shake, dislodging his hand, and stepping back as I hugged my laptop bag to my chest.

Although I had no need to defend myself from John, his appearance at this moment brought up too many memories of just how hard I'd looked for someone to fill the void created by what happened with Boone. And here I was, already falling for Boone again. Hell, I'd taken the dive myself and dragged him with me.

"I'm sorry," John said, looking so ridiculously sincere I actually had to fight back a laugh. "I screwed things up with you, Grace. If I could do it all over again, I'd get it right this time and appreciate what I had with you."

"Thanks, John." I honestly didn't know what else to say.

"I don't suppose you'd give me that chance," he said. This time his smile deepened, and he dipped his head low, staring directly into my eyes.

"Oh, for Christ's sake, John. We're not doing this again. I have absolutely no interest."

John shrugged easily. "Can't fault a guy for trying. I just might not give up, Grace."

"John, forget it. Please. Have a nice day," I

said as I shook my head, turning away and walking quickly down the hallway.

Hell if I knew why John wanted a second chance. I supposed he was bored, or perhaps he'd burned through too many bridges.

I kicked him to the curb mentally and settled in for my meeting. As I drove back to Stolen Hearts Valley that afternoon, I told myself John had done me a small favor. He'd reminded me why I needed to not to be stupid about anything. Although I didn't think Boone was anything like John, he had more thoroughly broken my heart.

I doubted anyone could break my heart as wholly as Boone had. I wanted to learn from my own mistakes. With that in mind, I resolved to be careful.

Boone knocked on my door that night. I opened it to find him there with takeout and a bottle of my favorite red wine from Lost Deer Winery. Of course, I couldn't resist and spent yet another night tangled up in his arms.

Chapter Twenty-Four

BOONE

"Hell if I know," I muttered, running a hand through my hair and kicking my heel against the wall behind me.

Dawson chuckled. "You'd better know, dude. If there's one thing I've figured out about relationships, it's that you have to know how you feel and talk about it."

Wade drained the water bottle in his hand, tossing the empty bottle into the bin nearby and rolling his eyes. "Oh, so you're in your first relationship ever, and now you're a fucking expert?"

Dawson wasn't even flustered. "I am. At least about knowing you have to communicate."

"How did I get lucky enough to be the

recipient of your unsolicited advice?" I queried.

We were waiting for our crew superintendent for a team meeting. For some damn reason, Dawson decided this was the time to ask for a personal update on my status with Grace. Considering that I wasn't too clear on what Grace wanted me to discuss openly with our shared friends, I had my hesitations to begin with. That said, I'd been direct with the guys that I intended to get Grace back once and for all this time.

Dawson shrugged. "Evie's worried about Grace. They're besties, you know?"

"Of course I know, dude. I went to high school with them."

Dawson nodded. "Exactly. I'm sure you know Evie'll kick my ass if you hurt Grace again. And, for God's sake, don't put us in a situation where we have to choose sides. I don't even wanna think about that."

Wade chuckled. "Seeing as Grace hardly talked to Boone for almost a year and we managed, it'll be fine."

I looked to Lucas, who'd been quiet thus far during this exchange. "Anything to offer?" I teased.

Lucas arched a brow. "Not much. Although Dawson is right."

"About what?"

"It's my experience women don't appreciate it when you're vague about your feelings."

"I'm not being vague," I protested. "I'm not sure what Grace wants right now. If I could get away with it, I'd ask her to marry me tomorrow. I think if I pull that, she'll tell me I'm crazy. It's only been a few days since Diana showed up and made me look like an asshole."

"Yeah, but you sorted that out right quick," Jackson chimed in.

Thank God for small favors. Diana had taken a plane back to Colorado. I was still puzzled as to why she flew all the way here to try to cry on my shoulder. My mother had suggested it was just emotional confusion. Whatever the hell it was, I hoped that was the last I saw of her.

"Since it's a group vote at this point, you might as well tell me what you think," I said, glancing at Walker.

Walker looked up. "I am *not* the man to ask about relationships."

"Uh, okay then, thanks."

Dawson interjected, "Just don't fuck it up. Otherwise, I'll be fielding interference with Evie. She's super protective of Grace."

———

The following evening, I leaned back in my chair at Lost Deer Bar, letting my eyes scan around the space. The night wasn't too busy yet, but the only person I was looking for was Grace. I'd spent my day off at my mother's house, working on the deck I was rebuilding for her. When Dawson had texted to invite me to meet him and some of the guys here, I'd decided to take him up on the invite. I figured if Evie was around, so was Grace.

Whether it was magnetism or just plain life, Grace walked in the back door. If a heart could smile, mine did. Although only a wall separated us at the duplex, I hadn't been able to see her for three nights in a row between her work schedule and mine. I was impatient to see her.

I didn't realize I was standing and striding to meet her until her eyes widened slightly when I stopped in front of her. "Hey, sugar," I said, leaning down to drop a kiss on her mouth. She turned away at the last second, leaving my kiss to land on her cheek.

"What are you doing, Boone?" she whispered.

Straightening, I smiled. "Saying hello. Is that a problem?"

Grace's lips tightened, and she lifted a shoulder in a small shrug. "Maybe. I'm not quite ready for the whole world to know about us."

Frustration burned in my brain and chest, and I wanted to shake her—to remind her that with us, it was something different, something special. To tell her that maybe it had all gone horribly wrong once upon a time, but this time we would get it right. I beat back all of it and stayed silent.

I knew, I fucking knew, having Diana show up out of the blue like that sure as hell hadn't helped matters. I sensed Grace was still picking her way through the rubble of our past and everything that had happened to each of us in the interim.

She looked away when Evie's voice rang out nearby, laughing at something Dawson said as he tugged her close to his side.

"Grace."

Her eyes bounced back to mine, a hint of guardedness contained there. It occurred to me just now that except for when we were tangled up together skin to skin and twined like vines around each other, that guarded look was always there. I wasn't entirely sure if it was just me that she didn't trust, or life and the bitter lessons and stinging scars left behind.

"Please don't shut me out."

Even over the low cacophony of sounds in the bar, I heard Grace take a deep breath, her shoulders rising and then curling forward slightly as they fell, almost as if to protect her heart.

"I'm not. You'd know if that was happening. I did that when you first came back." Her lips twisted in a bitter smile.

I wanted to reach for her and fold her into my arms, reminding her that we were finding our way back to each other. But I didn't.

At that moment, Walker came through the back door at the bar, nodding in greeting. Lucas, Valentina, and Lucas's sister, Jade, were right behind him.

They paused beside us. "Room at the table for a few more?" Lucas asked.

"Always," Dawson replied as he shifted his chair over to make room.

Acutely aware of Grace's nearness, my fingers practically itched with the urge to catch her hand in mine as we stopped by the table. I managed to refrain, relieved when Grace didn't go out of her way to sit away from me.

"How about a pitcher of beer?" Dawson

asked the table at large as we settled into our chairs.

"Y'all get whatever you want, but I'm sticking with water because I'm on call tonight," I replied.

"Same," Walker added.

"Not much sense in coming out to a bar if you can't even drink," Jade commented with a subtle roll of her eyes.

Lucas chuckled at my side. "There's always good food."

Jade, who I didn't know too well, cast her brother a sharp look. "True."

"Who isn't on call?" Dawson asked after a few others declared they were passing on beer.

"Looks like just you and me," Lucas offered with a laugh.

"All right, then, I guess I'll take a glass of the house draft," Dawson said, glancing up at the waitress.

The waitress circled the table and took orders.

"Be right back," Grace said as she pushed her chair back and stood. "Restroom break."

My eyes tracked her as she strode across the room. "Staring hard enough?" Evie's voice came from my side.

My eyes fell off Grace when she turned

into the hallway that led to the restrooms, and I looked at Evie. "Maybe."

She pursed her lips, one brow rising in a dark slash. "I think you mean to do right by Grace, but just know I'll kick your ass if you don't," she said pointedly.

Dawson leaned around her, not even bothering to hide the fact that he had overheard her. "See?"

"See what?"

"I told you I'd have to answer to Evie," he countered.

I shook my head as I laughed softly. "Evie, you don't need to worry. I think my heart is more at risk of getting broken than Grace's."

Evie's sharp gaze searched mine before she let out a soft sigh. "You might be right. Trust doesn't come so easy for Grace."

"Point taken. Any suggestions?"

"Just be patient."

"That's not really a suggestion, babe," Dawson offered wryly.

Evie nudged him with her elbow. "Maybe not, but I don't have anything better to offer." Her gaze scanned the room, and she said abruptly, "Oh shit."

"Damn, girl. What'd I do now?" Dawson teased, his tone light but puzzled.

"Nothing."

I followed Evie's gaze to see a man stopping beside Grace as she came out of the back hallway where the restrooms were. I didn't even know who the guy was, but my gut tightened.

"What's up?" Dawson pressed.

"It's John," she said, her voice low.

When my gaze slid sideways, I collided with Evie's gaze. She shrugged, as if to herself. "You probably never met John. He's the asshole who fucked around on Grace behind her back when they were dating."

Dawson looked from Evie over to the man in question, offering only, "Oh."

"What the hell is he doing here?" I asked, anger jolting through me.

"Your guess is as good as mine," Evie said.

When I saw the man reach out and lightly touch Grace's elbow, I stood without thinking. Grace jerked her elbow away as if she'd been shocked. There were enough people around that there wasn't far for her to go when she tried to step away. When he leaned forward to talk to her, her lips tightened.

I was across the bar fast, practically skidding to a stop at Grace's side. Her eyes lifted to mine, her brow knitting as she looked at me in confusion. "Everything okay?" I asked.

John looked me up and down. "She's fine. We're having a conversation if you don't mind."

"I think Grace might mind," I said, sliding my hand over her shoulders and down her spine as I stepped closer.

"Who the hell are you?" John asked, lifting his chin and nudging it toward me.

John had a smooth vibe to him, and I didn't doubt for a second he was used to getting whatever he wanted when it came to women. I didn't know if it was jealousy chewing me up, fury that this guy would dare to screw around behind Grace's back, or my own frustration with Grace trying to set boundaries with me, and then this idiot showing up. Nevertheless, I was determined to chase this asshole away.

"This is Boone," Grace said, pointlessly introducing us, "And this is John." She gestured to him.

John actually had the audacity to smirk. "Ah, Boone."

Grace narrowed her eyes at him. "What the fuck, John?"

"What? You gave me shit for having a different definition of exclusive from you when this is the guy who dumped you with no explanation," he said, gesturing in my direction.

Once again—because Grace had that effect on me—I acted without thinking. Stepping right to him, I looked down. "You don't know the half of it, you fucking asshole. You screwed around on her." I gave him a hard shove when he started to laugh. I ignored Grace calling my name. Because now I was just fucking pissed. No man could screw around on Grace behind her back and then laugh about it, not in front of me.

After another shove, when I knocked him off balance, John tried to straighten and actually threw a punch. The little fucking punk. He was a pretty boy if I ever saw one. Perhaps I was even more irate to realize that Grace had actually once seen something in this guy.

I had him by the collar and was lifting him up just as I heard Lucas's voice right behind me. "Fuck it. Let it go, Boone. You're making a scene, man."

Walker came up on my other side and grabbed my arm, his grip tight. They intervened in the nick of time because one of the bartenders was approaching us. By the time they could see what was going on, I had let go of John's collar. I gave him a last long look. "Fuck off."

With a glare, John spun away, muttering something under his breath.

"Everything okay?" The bartender asked, glancing amongst the group of people surrounding us.

"It's all good," Walker offered, his tone firm and authoritative.

I watched as John stalked down the back hallway and shook my arm loose from Walker's grip. I let out a ragged sigh and glanced his way. "Thanks, man. You too," I added, looking at Lucas on my other side.

"No problem," Lucas said, his tone dry.

Walker nodded and turned. "Be back," he said. "Need a bathroom break myself." I suspected he was going to check to make sure John left and I resisted the urge to follow.

The group broke apart, leaving me standing there with Grace. She looked up at me, nothing but annoyance in her expression. "What the hell, Boone?"

"Grace, that asshole screwed around on you, and he thinks it's funny."

"Maybe so, but I can take care of myself, Boone," she said, each word enunciated clearly. Two bright red spots crested on her cheeks as she stared at me.

"Grace, I know you can take care of yourself, but..."

She shook her head sharply. "Whether you like it or not, I don't need you to fight every fight for me. As John pointed out—even if you don't like the source—your record with me isn't much better."

I felt as if she had stuck a cold, icy knife right through my heart. "Grace, you know what happened now."

"I know. I do, but that didn't make it hurt any less when it happened. I don't need you to go all caveman on me. I wanted to take things slow, and instead, you're acting like we're a done deal."

At that, she spun away, hurrying out the back door to the parking lot. I started to go after her, only to get yanked to a stop by a hand on my elbow. When I looked over my shoulder, I found Evie there. She might be small, but she was strong and forceful.

"What?" I snapped. "If you don't mind, I'd like a chance to talk to Grace.

My gut was churning, and I felt the situation spiraling out of my control. Evie shook her head. "If you know her the way you did once, you know she wants space right now. Give it to her."

Staring at Evie, I leaned my head back and sighed. Fuck. Leveling my gaze with hers again, I added, "You're probably right. But—"

"Boone, she knows. Just give her some time."

I felt my jaw clenching and deliberately took a slow breath, trying to let the tension go. "Fine," I finally said. "I'm not gonna chase after her, Evie."

Evie loosened her grip on my arm, her hand falling away. Although my words to Evie were truthful, I didn't know how much tolerance I had for waiting. I had used up most of it this last year trying to give Grace a chance to come around. I was frankly relieved when we got an emergency call out. I needed something to keep me occupied.

Chapter Twenty-Five

GRACE

I took a bite of the cinnamon roll and let out a moan. "Oh my God," I said as a chewed, not even caring how rude that was. "Your cinnamon rolls are the best, Nancy."

Nancy smiled, patting my shoulder as she passed the table. "You look like you needed one this morning, hon. That one's on the house."

Wake & Bake Café was bustling. It was only six in the morning, but the early morning crew was out in force. In between bites of the buttery cinnamon deliciousness, I sipped my rich coffee and scanned the room. The café had soft cream colored walls and tall windows that let in plenty of sunlight to cast a warm glow on the wide plank hardwood floors. It was a warm, open space. I contemplated that Nancy had noticed I wasn't in the best mood.

After that stupid scene the other night at the bar, I'd gone home and sent a few glares over at the wall that separated my side of the duplex from Boone's. Between running into John twice within the last week and Boone's caveman act, I was annoyed.

As annoyed as I was, one thing had crystallized in my mind in the last few days. I was over John, well and truly. Not that I had ever fallen for him the way I had fallen for Boone, but all that was left were the stings to my pride.

More than that, I was annoyed with myself. When Boone had first moved back to Stolen Hearts Valley, I had promised myself every which way I could that I wouldn't let myself be as vulnerable as I had before. Oh, how foolish I was. I was coming to discover I'd never fallen out of love with Boone.

My heart was raw and beating outside of my chest when it came to him. Hence, my need to create a little space and get my bearings. The old humiliation of the way I had simply felt dropped by him before was still echoing whenever I thought about it. I'd felt tossed into thin air and spinning with nowhere to land because I hadn't expected to fall. Even though no one quite knew just how much it hurt—except perhaps him—I didn't want to feel this vulnerable this quickly. Not again.

Meanwhile, there he was, roaring back and ready to stake his claim publicly. My God, he'd practically started a fight with John. It was too many humiliations colliding in one interaction. Because everybody knew what John did.

"Morning, dear," my mother's voice came over my shoulder.

Glancing up, I managed something resembling a smile. "Morning, Mom."

I gestured to the chair across from me with some internal reluctance. It wasn't that I didn't want to see my mother, but she knew me too well, and she was way too perceptive.

She already had a cup of coffee in hand when she slipped into the chair across from me with a smile. "Well, you look a little glum," she said, cocking her head to the side.

I shrugged. "Maybe so." Much as I didn't want to discuss relationships with my mother, I figured I would ask her one thing. She might not like it, but I was going for it.

"How did you handle it when you found out dad was cheating on you?"

My mother, her usual unflappable self, let out a soft sigh. She took a sip of her coffee, and I could tell she was considering her response. After a moment, she shook her head slightly. "Love is complicated. As I've watched you over the last few years, my biggest regret is that I think it affected you as much as it did me."

Puzzled, I asked, "What do you mean?"

I took the last bite of my cinnamon roll, relieved for the delicious distraction of butter, sugar, and cinnamon that briefly overtook my senses. I was a stress eater, and I was seriously stressed at the moment.

My father's infidelity had always been disconcerting for me. I'd loved my father, and yet, I still harbored a kernel of anger and disillusionment. A brief affair and him temporarily moving out in the aftermath had been the very thing that almost blew apart my parents' marriage.

"Look, your father and I loved each other, and we had an imperfect marriage, which, I dare say, everyone has. We chose to get back together after everything that happened simply because I understood how it came to be. I forgave him."

"Okay. What do you mean about it affecting me? I mean, aside from the obvious."

"I think you were so disillusioned by our separation and later finding out he had an affair. Yes, it hurt my pride, but trust me, there are worse things. Your father was a flawed man, and I'm a flawed woman. He loved you dearly, and I still do. I also still miss him. I worry about its effect on you because circumstances unfortunately reinforced your distrust. What happened with Boone broke your heart."

I started to shake my head, and my mother leveled me with a forceful and knowing stare. "Pretending it didn't isn't going to help anyone. You never stopped loving him as far as I can tell."

"Mom, it just..."

"I'm glad he came back, and you finally got the whole story. You two were so young back then. You have every right to be hurt, but now you can understand the perspective. He was young, confused, and I would imagine, quite scared. In the middle of it all, his father got sick. Talk about muddying the waters of his emotional fortitude."

Only my mother would use the term emotional fortitude. I eyed her and nodded slowly. "I do understand it, I just—" Pausing, I shrugged.

"The stage is set for you not to have faith.

Your image of your father was shattered when you found out what happened. That wasn't helpful."

"The gossip certainly wasn't," I offered with a small shrug.

"Well, Harriet most definitely didn't need to blather the way she did," my mother said, pursing her lips tightly.

She was referencing an old acquaintance who had since passed away, the very woman who let it slip that my dad had an affair when I was younger. I was in college at the time and home on Christmas break. She was a little tipsy at the holiday party and babbled about a few too many town secrets.

"My entire point was to note that life is complex, and what you see happening without context can make it impossible to understand. Then, you dated John. I never liked him," my mother said sharply.

"I know you didn't. I've told you many times since we broke up that you were right."

Somehow I'd lost track of my original point in asking my mother about this. "So I have issues with trust. So what? I'm joining legions of women in that regard."

"And? Plenty of men have had women do hurtful things to them. Take Boone, for example." He had plenty of reasons not to trust women after what he went through with Diana. I didn't even bother to ask how my mother knew the whole story, but I was confident she did.

"Either you give love a chance again, or you don't. I've seen the way Boone looks at you. I know he would never hurt you. All he did wrong before hinged on the fact that he was too young to have enough sense to tell you what was going on."

Absorbing my mother's observation, I took a sip of coffee, that old anxiety spinning in my chest. It was *so* freaking hard for me to trust. And yet, here was Boone, barreling into my heart again.

Before I could reply, my mother skipped topics. She did that, often. "Speaking of how much Boone cares about you, how are your headaches? He hasn't said a word."

I laughed softly. "Yeah, he mentioned you asked him to keep an eye on me. You're not going to believe it, but I think it was my birth control pills. I switched to an IUD, and I haven't had one since. However, I was only getting them every few weeks, so we need to wait a while to say for sure."

"It's that simple? How come they didn't mention it sooner?"

"Probably because I should've checked with my OB/GYN first."

My mother smiled brightly. "That would be a huge relief if that's all it is."

"You're telling me."

After sipping her coffee, my mother asked, "So how have your classes been going?"

My doctoral program was a part-distance program, and I occasionally spent weekends in Asheville for on-campus classes. "Actually, I head up there this afternoon. I won't be back until Sunday."

"Would you mind running a few errands for me?"

"Of course not."

I left Stolen Hearts earlier than I planned to take care of my mother's errands before my classes. As it was, I never got a chance to see Boone before I left and thought perhaps that was a good thing. Much as I wanted to see him, I needed some emotional clarity, and only time and space could give me that.

Chapter Twenty-Six

BOONE

I felt the rock slide and fall above me, its descent silent. Yet, I could feel it coming right when it struck my shoulder. Hard. My voice pierced the darkness, a gruff shout of pain.

"You okay?" Walker called.

We were scaling a cliff in the darkness with floodlights to illuminate the area. Because for the thousandth time, some idiot had taken a slick corner on a winter road in the mountains too fast and hurtled through the guardrail.

I looked up into the lights angled over the cliff face for our team. I met Walker's eyes, where he was situated a few feet above me on a little outcropping. My shoulder stiffened as the sharp pain of the rock striking me receded. "I'm okay," I bit out, relieved I was in a harness with my feet pressed against the rock face.

"You got this?" Walker asked.

I couldn't see his eyes very well. Although we had floodlights shining down from above to assist us, the light was glaring and cast long shadows in the dark, rainy night. Only minutes within receiving this call out, the soft, icy drizzle falling outside had picked up its pace, making a dicey rescue even more questionable.

"I think so," I said. "Just need to get a little further down."

Wade was at the top, feeding rope down to Walker, who was then feeding it down to me. Jackson was already below me, working to free one of the two passengers out of the vehicle. Fortunately, he had already ascertained that they both appeared okay, beyond minor injuries.

With Walker steadily lowering me, I bounced further down the cliff, my feet coming to rest on a ledge where the car was cradled at the bottom of this embankment.

"How's it looking?" I asked Jackson as I picked my way in the darkness around where the vehicle had landed.

"All right." Jackson's reply was followed by a grunt.

I rolled my shoulder, testing it to find that it still ached, but my range of motion hadn't been affected.

"What do you need?" I stopped at his side, peering inside the vehicle.

"Hey, man," the driver slurred.

"If you could help me prop this door open, we should be able to get them both out on this side," Jackson explained, nudging the door in question with his knee.

The passenger rolled his head to the side, his eyes glassy. "My leg is fucking killing me," he muttered.

"We'll have you out in just a few," I said. I reached inside the window to pull the door latch open. Meanwhile, Jackson curled his hands around the frame. Between the two of us pulling, the door finally gave way and opened abruptly.

The next few moments passed quickly as Jackson and I checked on the driver and passenger before moving them. The driver had a broken arm, and the passenger had a nasty gash on his forehead and on his leg above his knee.

"We'll have to make sure they do the head

injury protocol at the hospital," I murmured to Jackson.

Jackson nodded before radioing up to the guys waiting at the top of the cliff. More of our crew rappelled down to help us get the guys up to the top of the cliff in safety harnesses. The ambulance was already waiting.

I was the last to come up, and Walker called down to check on me as he gathered the slack in the climbing rope. "Your shoulder holding up okay?"

"I'm good. I'm sure I'll have a bruise and be sore tomorrow," I called in return.

I opened my mouth to say something else when I heard him call, "Watch out!"

When the car had careened through the guardrail, it hit the loose gravel and rocks at the top of this cliff. Another rock came crashing down when I looked up. It didn't seem too big until it clocked me on the side of the head. Everything went black.

BOONE

A beeping sound woke me, and I rolled my head to the side, confused about where I was.

"What the hell?" I asked abruptly as I sat up. The simple act of speaking and moving sent a sharp pain through my head.

"Take it easy, Mr. Reeves," a man's voice reached me from across the room.

Befuddled, I collapsed against the pillows and looked around the room, taking in the white walls, the machine beeping beside me, and the hospital bed. "What the hell am I doing in the hospital?"

I glanced down to see an IV in my arm. The lights were dim, so I presumed it was in the middle of the night. The man finished doing whatever he was doing over at the sink mounted against the wall. Turning, he strode to the side of my bed, quickly tapping a button to look at a screen mounted on a wheeled cart nearby. "Your vitals look good." The man's eyes scanned me. He had dark brown hair sprinkled with silver and grayish-blue eyes.

"Are you my doctor? If so, can you get me the hell out of here?"

The man shook his head. "No can do, I'm afraid. I'm one of your nurses. Brent Carlson. You won't be checking out because it's too early. The doctor on duty tomorrow morning will take a look at everything and decide whether you can be cleared for discharge. Meanwhile, how are you feeling?"

By Brent's demeanor, I'd have had no idea it was dark outside. He was far too chipper and cheerful for that. "Can I just leave?" I pressed.

"I'm sorry, but no."

"But I feel fine," I protested as I began to set up, wincing at the sharp, throbbing pain on the side of my head.

"Yeah, you look like you feel fine," Brent observed dryly.

"What the hell happened, and what time is it?"

Brent turned slightly in his chair, opening

a laptop behind him on the counter on the wall. "It's going on five a.m. Let's get you some ibuprofen." I wasn't going to turn that down, so I nodded. He filled a paper cup from a pitcher of water on the table beside my bed and handed me two pills.

After I gulped down the ibuprofen, he finally answered my question. "I don't know what you remember, but you got clocked pretty good on the head with a rock late last night during a rescue operation."

As I stared at him, flickers of recognition filtered in. "I remember everything but that part."

"I would imagine. It knocked you out completely. You didn't regain consciousness until after you were in the ambulance."

"We've been checking you every two hours since you got here and waking you up. It's part of the head injury protocol."

"Damn. Any of my crew around?"

Brent tilted his head. "It's not even five a.m. I'm sure they would've stayed here in solidarity, but I assured them you were fine. They went home to a well-deserved night of rest. If you need company, I'm here for now."

"I think I can handle it."

"Are you waiting on anyone to visit?" he asked.

My mind swooped in the direction of Grace, and I wondered if she even knew I was here.

"What's that look for?"

I slid my gaze back to Brent. "Shouldn't you be working?"

"I am," he said brightly. Most of the patients are still asleep. Do tell."

"I don't know if I have a girlfriend," I said with a sigh, thinking the dull ache in my head was easier to bear than the sight of Grace storming out of the bar last week. She'd been gone for the last two nights. I'd only found out she was at her weekend classes in Asheville from Evie.

"Oh, darn. You're straight."

That got a chuckle from me. "Yeah, sorry to disappoint you."

"No worries. My boyfriend would think you're cute too. Anyway, I love giving relationship advice to strangers. I've also found that straight men can be stupid when it comes to romance, so perhaps I can help."

I laughed, ignoring the pain in my head. "Well, the woman I'd like to call my girlfriend accused me of going caveman last week. She said she wanted to slow things down."

"Oh dear, caveman? You pulled that stunt?"

"It all made sense at the time. Some guy who screwed around on her when they dated showed up, and he laughed when I called him out."

"Hmm. She didn't appreciate it, I take it?"

"No. And we're just kind of getting back together."

Next thing I knew, I spilled the whole messy tale to Brent in my quiet hospital room. He was a good listener. He also told me he didn't think Grace would have let anything happen between us if she didn't care.

"Okay then, what do I do?"

This was what it had come to. Me asking an almost-stranger in the hospital for relationship advice before the sun came up.

Brent looked at the clock mounted on the wall at the foot of my bed. "Does she even know you're here?"

"Seeing as I didn't even know why I was here at first, I have no fucking clue if she knows I'm here."

Brent nodded slowly. "Good point. Well, I say you call her."

"Now?"

"What time does she normally get up?"

"Probably six or seven."

"Seven. It's safe."

"And what?"

"Am I gonna have to give you a script?"

Leaning my head back into the pillows, I let out a sigh. "No. I just want to skip through this to the part where she trusts me again, and it's all okay."

"It sounds like some of her baggage has nothing to do with you, so you might have to be patient. Tell her you know you were an idiot, you know you overshot, and tell her you fucking love her. I bet you haven't, have you?"

"I was trying not to rush," I mumbled sheepishly.

"You have to walk that fine line between not pressuring her, but letting her know precisely how you feel and how important she is to you. If she's a woman who has trouble with trust—and based on everything you told me she has plenty of reason for that—then you've got to stack the deck in your favor as far as giving her a reason to trust you. That means telling her how you feel and letting her know you're there when she's ready."

"Why should I trust you on all this? You don't even date women."

Brent's brows hitched up as he pinned me with a look. "Seriously? The worst people to ask for dating advice are straight men."

At that moment, his pager beeped. After a quick glance at it, he looked back at me. "I actually need to check on someone. How's your head feeling by the way?" he asked, his demeanor shifting to all business in a matter of seconds.

Lifting my hand, I wiggled it back and forth. "Better. What's the protocol?"

"If you fall asleep, we wake you up every two hours until you stay awake. When you go home, you'll need someone to monitor you until you've passed the twenty-four-hour window. That'll be later tonight. You needed stitches on the side there."

"I did?" I lifted my hand to find my hair buzzed short on one side.

"Yeah, I'd recommend a full trim. It's looking like a haircut gone wrong," he said as he stood. "I'll check back by seven to make sure you're awake to give Grace a call."

Chapter Twenty-Eight

GRACE

It was foggy this morning. Main Street in Stolen Hearts Valley was shrouded in mist as I came to a stop and parked my car across the street from Wake & Bake Café. I was trying to ignore the yearning that just wouldn't quit for Boone. I'd gotten home from Asheville late last night and wrestled with the disappointment of finding his truck gone. It had now been five days since I'd seen him. It felt like far more than that.

The truth was I loved him, and I'd never stopped. I marveled at how well I'd avoided facing this truth for years. While there'd been enough chemistry with John at the beginning to push me into thinking I could move on, it had dissipated quickly. John had only added another layer to my issues of mistrust with men and left my pride stinging. *So not worth my time.*

Mulling over my conversation with my mother had me tossing and turning in bed last night. Try as I might this last week, taking a break from Boone hadn't been easy. Matters were, of course, made far worse by the fact that he was my immediate neighbor. We shared a wall, and as I stood in my kitchen every night, I wondered what he was doing.

Before I left for Asheville, to help me stay distracted, I'd worked myself to the bone. I'd actually been relieved another waitress was on vacation because there were plenty of shifts for me to cover. Even Dani had given me the side-eye, pointing out that, while she appreciated me picking up the slack in the schedule, she knew I was doing it to avoid Boone. I'd ignored her, and she'd been too damn busy to do anything about it. Then, my reprieve came by way of my graduate classes. Between my work schedule and him being gone for a few days for an out of town training exercise with the first responder crew, I had five days to myself to run laps in my brain. I'd eventually come to the conclusion that avoidance wasn't solving anything, and I missed Boone.

The piercing sense of his absence echoed so much that I couldn't bear to ignore it any longer. This morning, I couldn't help but notice his truck wasn't home. It was bothering me.

I hoped I'd finally have a chance to talk to him later today. Shouldering through the doorway into Wake & Bake Café, I sighed as the warm, coffee-scented air surrounded me. With a glance around, I saw the other early morning customers sitting at tables reading and chatting. Even though it wasn't even six a.m. yet, there was a short line at the counter.

When I reached the front of the line, Nancy smiled. "What'll it be, dear?"

"Just black coffee. The strongest you've got."

Nancy nodded and turned to begin prepping my coffee. "You hear about Boone Reeves?"

My heart jolted. "What about him?"

"Oh, I thought you'd have known before anyone else since he's your neighbor. He got hurt last night during a rescue. A boulder hit him right in the head. I guess he's going to be all right, but last I heard he was at the hospital."

"What?"

I felt as if I were buzzing all over, fear and anxiety churning in my stomach as I stared at Nancy. She lowered her hands as she handed over my cup of coffee. "Are you okay, hon? It sounds like he'll be fine."

I shook my head. "I have to go. I'm sorry, I'll pay for this later," I called over my shoulder as I dashed out of the café.

It was good I had the roads in Stolen Hearts Valley memorized because I drove like a crazy woman straight to the hospital through the foggy, misty morning. The sun was barely puncturing the clouds when I skidded to a jerking stop in the parking lot, my tires squealing a little on the damp pavement at the hospital.

Slamming the car door behind me, I raced across the parking lot and through the doors. My purse got caught on the door handle, and I didn't even bother to pick it up as I ran to the reception desk.

The receptionist glanced up, all business when she smiled politely at me. "How can I help you?"

"I need to know where Boone Reeves is," I blurted out.

"Are you family?"

"No, but I have to see him."

She gave me a searching look before she clicked on the computer screen. "Ma'am, I can't release any patient information without explicit consent."

"Is this yours?" A voice came from behind me.

Harried, I glanced over my shoulder to see a handsome man holding my purse. "Oh yes, I'm sorry," I said, reaching out. As he handed it over, my eyes scanned his nametag —Brent. "Brent, can you help me?"

The woman called from over my shoulder from behind the desk. "Ma'am, he cannot release private patient information either. Please have a seat, and we'll find out if you can be added to the approved visitor list. First, I need you to give me your name."

Brent cast a sympathetic look in my direction before turning toward her with a polite smile. I turned back to face Miss Protocol. "Fine. My name is Grace, Grace Lakes. I'm sure Boone will want to see me."

I didn't actually know if that was the case. I just knew that I needed to know he was okay. Preferably right this second.

When I turned back, Brent had vanished. "Dammit," I muttered to myself.

I couldn't say why, but I sensed he was a softer touch than Miss Protocol here. I heard her tapping on the screen and then lifting her phone. She said nothing though, so I didn't know what the hell was going on. She glanced up again, once again offering a bland, polite smile when she hung up. "I will definitely let you know as soon as I have an update. Please have a seat, ma'am."

"You don't need to call me ma'am," I snapped as I stomped away from her and sat down in one of the chairs in the waiting area across from her.

I quickly pulled out my phone, swiping on the screen and seeing Boone's last text when I tapped his name.

Hey Grace, I know you're pissed off. Please don't shut me out like this. I miss you.

I'd ignored that damn text for days and hadn't even allowed myself to open it. Until now, all I'd seen in the preview was *Hey Grace, I know you're pissed.*

My throat tightened. Sure, I had trust issues, and I needed to figure them out, but I knew there was only one man I wanted to figure them out with. That man was Boone.

If only because I wanted to make sure he saw it, I typed out a reply.

Hey, I hope you're ok. I'm waiting at the hospital, and Miss Protocol at the reception desk won't even tell me where you are or if you're ok. I miss you too, even if you're a caveman sometimes. xoxo

Slipping the phone back in my purse, I stood, too restless to sit down. Glancing around when I saw Miss Protocol was occupied, I strode quickly down the hallway, trying to remember where they had coffee. The last time I'd been here was years back when my father was sick. I let out a little sigh.

Whether I remembered it consciously, or my unconscious took me there, I found the coffee. Moments later, I was sipping on the much needed, but not-so-great coffee. I didn't even remember if I'd taken my coffee from Wake & Bake Café. My best guess was I'd left it in my car.

With this coffee, I didn't even think sugar could mask its prepackaged flavor. I had just taken another gulp when I heard the sound of movement behind me. Glancing back, I saw Boone. He wore a hospital gown and had an IV on a wheeled stand beside him. His head was shaved on one side, and a row of stitches was visible.

The subtle motion of the coffee in the thin paper cup alerted me to the tremor in my hands. I was frozen for a moment, my eyes scanning over him before I took several steps in his direction.

My heart was pounding so hard, every beat reverberated through my entire body. "Oh my God, Boone. Are you okay?" My voice sounded shaky as I suddenly rushed at him, closing the distance between us. I caught myself, stopping abruptly in front of him. "What are you doing? Aren't you supposed to be in your bed or something?"

My eyes scanned him rapidly, and I lifted a hand. I placed it incongruously on the wheeled IV stand, almost afraid to touch him anywhere.

"I'm fine," he murmured, his voice coming out just ragged enough that I thought he was deathly ill.

I pointed up at the stitches on the side of his head. "You cut your head." My voice sounded weird and jerky, and my hand shook when I held it up.

"I'm fine, baby," Boone said, taking a step closer and sliding an arm over my shoulder and down my back. He somehow managed to pull me close even though he was hooked up to an IV.

"You're not fine, Boone," I protested. For some strange reason, arguing over whether or not he was fine steadied me inside. "What happened?" I peered up at him, my heart squeezing and anxiety spinning tightly in my chest.

"We responded to an accident. I climbed down a cliff with Jackson and some of the other guys. The last thing I remember is looking up at Walker on the way up. Apparently, a good size rock fell and hit me on the head. I was just about to call you," he said, his hand sliding up and down my back in a soothing pass.

I didn't quite feel right that he was the one trying to comfort me, so I tried to take charge. "You need to go back to your room. Isn't there something about head injury protocol? Do that."

He let out a gruff laugh, pulling me against his chest. I took a breath and burrowed my face into his neck. He smelled like disinfectant. "Yeah, they already did that. I've been awake long enough. I guess someone will need to keep an eye on me until tonight, but I'm fine. I promise."

"Well then, why are you hooked up to an IV? Plus, they did a terrible job shaving your head," I murmured into his chest.

I looked up again, raising a hand to lightly trace my fingers along his shaved hairline just beside the stitches. It was a neat, tidy line of stitches, roughly three inches long. "Have you seen yourself?"

A smile kicked up at one corner of his lips. "Yep. It'll grow back."

"I can get you an appointment with my boyfriend to tidy up the other side," a voice said from the doorway.

Peering out from the shelter of Boone's embrace, I saw the same nurse who I thought might have been kinder than Miss Protocol.

Boone glanced over and smiled slightly. "Brent, this is Grace. She found me before I even called her." Brent stepped into the room, crossing toward us. Boone looked from me to him, adding, "He's been my nighttime nurse, the one who's been checking on me. Thank God I can deal with him."

I met Brent's eyes and smiled. "I found him even though Miss Protocol wouldn't tell me where he was. Now, can you help me get him back to his room? Because somehow, I don't think he's supposed to be wandering the halls."

Brent's brows hitched up. "Miss protocol, huh? Don't give her too hard of a time. She's just doing her job. And yes, I'd be glad to escort Boone back to his room. He absconded without telling any of us where he was going," Brent offered pointedly.

Boone—who was too cheerful by far, as far as I was concerned—chuckled as he turned to follow Brent out of the room and down the hallway while I followed. "My ibuprofen kicked in. Plus, you said I should be cleared to go soon.

Brent glanced over his shoulder. "*After* the doctor clears you. In the meantime, let's go to your room and check all your vitals before I unhook you from the IV."

While we were walking down the hall, Dawson's voice carried to us. "Well, there you are." Looking back, I saw Dawson break into a jog to catch up to us. "The lady at the front wouldn't tell me a damn thing." He stopped beside us, where we had paused to wait in the hallway. "Looking good," he drawled with a nod at Boone's stitches.

Boone winked. "I needed another scar. Plus, when my hair grows in, this one won't show."

"Damn good thing," Dawson teased.

"How is this funny?" I demanded, looking between them.

"Because he's fine," Dawson said, his smile fading as he looked at me. "We weren't laughing last night. But, now that we know he's okay, we can tease him. This is how we cope."

I took in a shuddering breath and shook my head. "Fine." Looking to Brent, I added, "Let's get him to his room, so you can do whatever you need to do."

"I sure as hell don't want to stay any longer than I have to, so if you could speed this process up, that would be great," Boone chimed in.

"You're staying as long as they tell you to stay," I said sternly.

Dawson's brows hitched up. "Better listen to Grace."

As I followed them down the hallway and into the hospital room where Brent began the steps that would lead to Boone's discharge, I tried to get my heart to calm down. Although I'd been slowly circling this conclusion for weeks now, there was an urgency to my feelings now.

As painfully difficult as it was to let go and try to trust in Boone and what we had, either I scrambled up the courage to do so, or I regretted it for the rest of my life.

I loved him, and I didn't want to miss any more time with him. I was tired of trying to play it cool, tired of working so hard to keep my walls up because it kept me safe.

Somewhere along the way that morning, we had a brief few moments alone. This was after Dawson had departed, and a few other friends had checked in. Brent left the room with assurances that the doctor who'd already been by was signing off on Boone's discharge.

I glanced over to where Boone sat with his hips resting on the edge of the hospital bed. He had changed out of his hospital gown into a pair of jeans and a faded T-shirt, graciously delivered by Jackson after I gave him the keys to the duplex.

Boone was running his finger over the area where the IV needle had punctured his skin on the inside of his forearm. He looked up, catching my eyes. "No bruising. Whoever put that in did a clean job."

Caught in his warm gaze, emotion tightened in my chest and my heart swelled, beating wildly. "I'm guessing that was Brent, huh?"

"Maybe," he replied as he looked at me across the space that separated us. I was standing by the windows, with my arms crossed tightly in front of my chest. As if drawn up by an invisible string, I turned, my arms falling loose as I closed the distance between us and stopped in front of him.

Boone rested his hands on my hips and pulled me in between his knees. "I love you," I whispered. I let it slip out, too tired of even trying to hold it at bay, much less trying to keep the truth from him.

His eyes swung to mine, the intensity in his gaze stealing my breath. "I never stopped loving you, Grace."

And then, he was pressing hot, open kisses on the side of my neck and proceeded to get a little bit naughty for hospital room protocol.

Chapter Twenty-Nine

BOONE

I leaned back into the cushions on the couch in Grace's living room. I rolled my shoulder experimentally, just testing to see how it felt. Although I didn't remember the rock hitting me on the head, I definitely remembered the one that whacked me on the shoulder.

My shoulder was sore, but it would be okay. Strangely, my head hurt less. Probably because I didn't move it all the damn time. Two days had passed since I was discharged after that night in the hospital, two days during which Grace fussed over me like crazy.

She approached from the kitchen with a tray that had a large pizza, specially made for me by Dani along with a beer from Lost Deer

Brewery. I'd had to have Brent call her to assure her it was okay for me to drink beer. I wasn't even taking anything more than ibuprofen, but she worried anyway.

She set the pizza down on the coffee table and handed me the beer. I immediately set it down, catching the hem of her shirt and tugging her close. "Come here."

She was wearing a loose T-shirt and a pair of sweatpants that swung around her ankles. There was nothing remarkable about what she was wearing, but I thought she was sexy as hell. Her hair was piled up in some sort of bun on top of her head with loose tendrils framing her face.

"I'm right here," she replied as she glanced down at me, brushing an errant lock of hair away from her forehead with the back of her wrist.

"No, I mean, come *here*." I snuck an arm around her hips to pull her down on my lap.

"Boone! What are you doing?"

When she wiggled, I held her firm. "Getting you right where I want you," I teased.

I knew she could feel the hard ridge of my arousal pressing against her bottom, and that was perfectly all right with me. I had a point to make.

"You're injured," she protested as she

turned to look at me, her cheeks flushed pretty and pink.

"I'm completely fine. Is it my hair? I thought Brent's boyfriend did a nice job of evening it out."

Grace giggled. "It's not your hair, and he did make it look much better," she said, lifting a hand and smoothing it over my close-cropped locks.

"Grace," I pleaded. "I've got you all to myself, and you're treating me like I'm fine china. They don't even think I'll have any residual effects from getting knocked out."

I gave her a little tug, and she fell against me. I pressed a kiss to the side of her neck, breathing in the sweet scent of her and reveling in the feel of her skin rising in goosebumps under my lips as I trailed hot kisses across her collarbone.

"Boone," she protested, rather weakly I might add. I knew I'd won when she let out a soft moan when I nipped the sensitive skin right behind her ear.

"Come on, sweetheart. I'll let you be on top," I murmured as I reached between her thighs.

"Not fair," she gasped as her hips arched reflexively into my touch.

I slid a hand up under her T-shirt, gratified to find she wasn't wearing a bra. I was even more gratified to discover her nipples puckered tightly as I cupped a breast and teased my thumb back and forth over one.

Once I sweet-talked her out of her clothes, I made quick work of mine. Despite her protests, I was perfectly capable of getting my shirt off and freeing my cock from my boxers.

"I promise I'll rest and just sit right here," I teased as I leaned over to catch one of her peaked nipples with my mouth, giving it a sharp suck and a nip with my teeth.

"You're nothing but trouble," she murmured as I snuck my hand back between her thighs to find her hot, wet, and ready for me.

Despite her protestations, she didn't resist, straddling me and rising up, her gaze flashing as I felt the sweet heat of her entrance tease the head of my cock.

"I'm nothing but *yours*," I said just as I gripped her hips and guided her down over me.

Much as I liked to think I had some control when it came to Grace, I had none. She shredded it. As her slick heat sheathed me, I let my head fall back into the couch pillows, letting out a rough groan.

It didn't take long before my release was

barreling towards me, spinning tighter and tighter inside as Grace cried out when I pressed my thumb over her clit. Her nipples jutted forward when she arched back, her entire body shattering. I let go, surrendering myself to her and to the rush of my release.

I was hers—body, heart, and soul.

EPILOGUE

Grace

Approximately 5 years later

"You have *got* to be kidding me," I said, hands on my hips as I stared up at Bruce. He let out a plaintive meow, his tail twitching from where he sat perched on the tree branch. "How the hell did you get up there? And Boone isn't home, so I don't even know what I'm gonna do." I eyed Bruce, considering my options.

Bruce came to us as a kitten when he was found wandering on the side of the road near Stolen Hearts Lodge. With Wayne having passed away peacefully in his sleep a few months prior, we hadn't hesitated to take in

Bruce. Since Wayne had been named after Bruce Wayne, we stuck with the tradition and gave Bruce the other half of the name. We'd have to get more creative if we ever got another cat.

Even with the ladder, Bruce was out of my reach. I let out a sigh.

"Hey, sweetheart!" Boone called from behind me.

Turning back, my heart thumped hard, and a smile stretched across my face. "Perfect timing," I called as I approached him. "You're home a day early."

"Daddy!"

I watched as our son raced across the yard, bumping into his father's calves and flinging his arms around his knees. At one month past three years old, Adam was constantly on the move.

Boone swept Adam up into his arms, lifting him high and spinning him in a circle before he lowered him to rest on his hip.

"How ya doing, buddy?" Boone asked as he reached a hand toward me, gesturing for me to come closer.

Adam launched into one long run-on sentence, ending with "...and then my spider toy got torn by Bruce."

Boone pressed a kiss to Adam's forehead.

"Well, if that's the worst thing that happened while I was gone, that's not too bad."

Boone pulled me close, his arm sliding down my back and coming to rest at the dip of my waist. I glanced up just as he looked my way, his warm gaze catching me. "And how about you?"

"Bruce is in the tree again, and I'm glad you got home early."

With Adam still in his arms, he dusted a kiss on my temple and caught my lips with his briefly, the promise contained there enough to send my belly spinning in flips.

"You have a job to do," Adam announced, bouncing his heels against Boone's leg.

"Sure looks like it. Why don't I go ahead and take care of that?"

He released me and eased Adam to the ground, striding into the shed along the side of the house and returning with the ladder.

Not much later, we were in the kitchen. I made pancakes while Boone filled us in on why he got back a day early. Short answer: he and Wade drove through the night like idiots. As it was, he was exhausted, but I wasn't going to complain. He was back home, and that was pretty much all that mattered.

I set down a plate in front of him and another in front of Adam. He'd been chattering nonstop to Boone. "Oh, before I forget. We've got the guys coming to fix the boiler this afternoon. I hoped to have it done before you got home, but you're early."

One of those dangerous smiles unfurled across Boone's face. Slow and sly and guaranteed to get me a little hot and bothered. "I don't mind. Just good to be home."

My heart pounded in my chest, and I took a breath, letting it out slowly. I had another surprise to share with Boone, but that would wait for later. For now, I'd bask in the fact that he was home.

Four years had passed, during which a lot had happened. Boone asked me to marry him late one afternoon when we were still living in the shared duplex. He'd paid rent all along, but it was a complete waste of money. His place was really nothing more than a glorified closet for him.

We still rented the duplex out, and it was a good source of passive income. We'd moved though. Boone built us a house, nestled into a bluff that looked out over Stolen Hearts Valley. I adored it.

It did, in fact, turn out that those migraines had been a side effect of my birth control pills. My IUD had served me well until it fell out, and Boone and I decided to take that as the chance to try to get pregnant. That had happened remarkably fast.

I'd finished my dissertation and taken a position at the local community college. I also still covered shifts at Stolen Hearts Lodge whenever Dani was in a pinch.

Meanwhile, Boone was still a first responder, but his position had expanded to doing trainings all over the country. He traveled every few months, and I missed him even when it was only a few days.

My attention was brought back to the moment by Bruce jumping on the table and swiping Adam's pancake.

"He took my pancake!" Adam exclaimed.

Boone caught my eye, fighting a grin before he glanced over at our son, his gaze completely somber. "He did. What shall we do about that?"

Bruce was tearing at it on the floor by the window, so the pancake was a lost cause. Adam sighed and looked up at me. "Do we have any left?"

After breakfast, while I was making a fresh pot of coffee, my mother arrived to pick up Adam for the day. The moment she was out the door, Boone came up behind me. He slipped his arms around my waist and dropped hot kisses along the sensitive skin right at the juncture of my neck and shoulder.

I shivered slightly and leaned my head back. "Aren't you tired?"

"Not too tired for this," he murmured right before he cupped my jaw lightly, angling my face so he could bring his lips to mine.

———

BOONE

I dropped my head into the dip of Grace's shoulder, still shuddering from my release. The thing was, I couldn't be away from Grace for any length of time without wanting her the moment I saw her again.

I prided myself on being a good father, but the hardest part was keeping my hands to myself when our son was around.

"Thank God your mom was already coming to pick Adam up," I commented when I lifted my head.

We were still in the kitchen. Because, yeah, I had it that bad for Grace. It was all about efficiency when I was this desperate for her. We happened to be standing in the kitchen the moment I got her alone. I was quite convinced kitchen counters were made for sex more than anything else. The height was just perfect. Grace's legs were curled around my hips. She relaxed them, letting them dangle off the counter as I brushed her hair back from her face.

She giggled and leaned forward to press a soft kiss to my lips. "I didn't plan it because of you. I figured it was best if he wasn't underfoot when the guys came today to work on the boiler."

I stepped back reluctantly, but aware we needed to be decent when the service guys came by. Grace hopped off the counter as I buttoned my jeans. "The timing is perfect. We'll get it taken care of before winter. You got anything else planned today?"

She shook her head. "I was going to go to the grocery store."

"We'll do that together and grab dinner out tonight."

I could tell she was mulling something over.

"What?" I asked.

Grace was tugging the stretchy cotton skirt she wore back down around her hips. She caught my eyes and rolled hers. "You're always messing up my clothes."

I grinned, not the least bit sorry. "Isn't that what clothes are for?"

"In our life, I guess so." Grace lifted her mug and took a sip.

It crossed my mind for the second time this morning that she was drinking tea.

"What's with the tea? I know you love your coffee. Don't tell me we're going to do some kind of cleanse."

Grace went quiet, her cheeks flushing slightly before a slow smile curled at the corners of her mouth.

"What is it?" I stepped closer to where she stood with her hips leaned against the counter.

"We three are on our way to being four."

My heart lunged to a rapid beat in my chest. "You're pregnant?"

Grace swallowed, biting her lip as she nodded. "Yep. My period was due two weeks ago, and I figured I might as well do a test just to see."

Joy exploded, and I lifted her in my arms, spinning around.

She squeaked. "Oh my God, Boone. I spilled my tea!"

When I felt a splash of the warm liquid hit my arm, I stopped spinning, and eased her down. "I think I have super sperm."

Grace burst out laughing. "Oh my God. Super sperm or not, I'm pregnant."

I sobered, resting my forehead against hers. "This is the best news."

"It happened awful fast."

We'd only decided to try again last month. So yeah, it was quick. I only hoped I wouldn't be the anxious wreck I was during her last pregnancy.

I murmured, "I love you, you know?"

"I think I do. I love you too."

Then, the woman who'd held my heart since she was just a girl leaned up and pressed a kiss to my cheek. Tugging once again on the heartstrings that tied us together.

———

TALK TO BOONE

Want to hear more from Boone? You can message with him on Facebook: Talk to Boone He might be nosy about what you think of his story. ;)

———

Thank you for reading Still Go Crazy - I hope you loved Grace & Boone's story!

Up next in the Swoon Series is If We Dare.

Walker is tall, dark, and hot, hot, hot. He's definitely not looking for love, but he does need a date - a fake date for a wedding.

When Walker rescues Jade from the dumpster—no need to wonder why—she figures she owes him a small favor, so she offers to be his date. Jade consider herself man-proof and can totally handle a weekend with Walker.

There are two problems. Walker didn't expect to want Jade, and Jade sure as hell didn't expect to want Walker. What's supposed to be a fake date starts to feel as real as the fire burning up the sheets.

Their romance is burning hot, emotional & oh-so-swoony!

Keep reading for a sneak peek!

Be sure to sign up for my newsletter for the latest news, teasers & more! Click here to sign up: http://jhcroixauthor.com/subscribe/

Jade

"Hey!" I called, my eyes trained on the jerk who was getting a little too handsy with a woman at the bar. I'd served her and her friends a few minutes ago, and tonight was her twenty-first birthday.

The woman in question, Megan something or other, tried to laugh it off, politely taking a few steps away. It was crowded in the bar tonight though, so there wasn't far for her to go. The man immediately closed the space between them.

"Hey!" I called, quickly lifting a section of the counter at the back of the bar, slipping out and aiming right for the group where they were standing.

Megan wasn't alone, but her friends were

tied up flirting. Striding up to the man, I tapped him on the shoulder. He turned back, a leer affixed to his face. "Oh, hey, hot bartender, what can I do for you?" he slurred.

I silently cursed the other bartender on duty tonight, Joe, who tended not to pay too much attention to just how drunk people were getting and continued to serve them. That was a problem for another evening though. Narrowing my eyes as I looked up at the lumbering jerk standing before me, I rested a hand on my hip. "Back the fuck off. It doesn't look like she appreciates your attention."

Megan's eyes met mine—I only knew her name because I'd carded her—a look of relief passing across her face. "Thank you," she mouthed.

"Since when do you speak for all women?" The man punctuated this sentence with a long burp, which got a few guffaws from his friends surrounding him.

Glancing around, I cast a sharp gaze. I had no problem throwing every single one of these guys out. "Like I said, back off. Consider this my last warning."

The asshole *still* didn't get it. He leaned down, getting a little too close to my face and slurred. "Fuck off. Get back behind the bar and serve my friends some drinks."

Perhaps I should've been afraid, but I wasn't. For starters, the bar back and Joe were around and nearby. I also had friends here tonight even if they didn't happen to be in this precise corner of the sprawling Lost Deer Bar where I was only covering a shift as a favor tonight.

"That does it. You're out of here," I said, gesturing over my shoulder toward the door as I reached for the guy's arm.

"Hell no! I'm not fucking leaving," he grumbled, reaching for poor Megan who was pinned against the wall at this point, doing her best to look invisible. He snatched her hand. Well, fuck it.

Ignoring the rumble of voices around me, I lifted my boot and kicked him right in the knee. I decided to go for that instead of his balls as a starting point. In the back of my mind, I was legitimately wondering where the hell my help was.

The guy cried out in pain. His broad square face turned a mottled red as he dropped Megan's hand—that was my goal, so I took that as a win—and stepped toward me. Next thing I knew, he'd grabbed me by the waist with both hands and heaved me in the air.

I didn't scare easy, but now a little bit of fear bolted through me. I was known for getting myself in a pickle here and there, and I just might've gone and done that now.

Before I could make a peep, a voice came over my shoulder her. "Put her down. Now."

Whoever spoke wasn't waiting. Next thing I knew, a hand shot out, slamming into the guy's elbow. Something happened at his knees too. He stumbled and cried out sharply. Just as I began to tumble loose from his hold, my savior caught me with one arm and pulled me against his side.

I glanced up into the face of Walker Flint. My body felt as if it had been touched by a live wire. With Walker holding me fast to his side with one arm, I wasn't going anywhere. I might not like it in my mind, my body thought it was fucking awesome. Walker was nothing but pure muscle and lean power as he held me close.

The jerk who'd grabbed me was still groaning about his knee, but gathered himself together enough to glare at Walker. "You fucking dick."

He made a move toward Walker who simply lifted one arm and grabbed him by the wrist. Whatever he did brought the man to his knees with a yelp.

"Now, you're gonna fucking leave before I kick your ass," Walker said.

His low, fierce words sent a sizzling thrill through me. I was *not* the kind of girl who got all hot and bothered over men being tough. And yet, here I was, my body nearly vibrating at the force of Walker's presence and my panties getting wet from the sound of his voice.

I stole another glance at him. I knew him because he worked with my older brother, and they were friends. Walker was hot. His face looked as if it had been carved from marble. He had strong cheekbones and a straight nose paired with a square jaw. He even had a dimple in his chin. To make matters worse, his lips were bold and sensual.

I didn't think I'd ever seen the guy crack a smile. His eyes were an icy silver. Ever since the first time I'd met Walker, we'd rubbed each other the wrong way. For God's sake, the man could not relax.

Not that I minded that issue just about now. He leveled his cool gaze at the guy's friends, adding, "Why don't y'all get the hell out of here? Sound like a plan?"

Whether it was the tone of his voice, or

the look in his eye, or the fact that whatever he'd done to the guy with a flick of his wrist had brought him to his knees, they took notice. After a loaded moment, the friends appeared to think Walker's suggestion was a good plan and started to shuffle out.

"Are we clear?" Walker asked, staring down at the guy on his knees.

"If you'll fucking let me go, I'll get the hell out of here."

Walker released the guy's wrist. "Fair enough. If I ever see you getting pushy with any woman who doesn't want it, I might not be so nice next time."

At that, the guy stood, stumbling on his way toward the door, which was blessedly close. Only then did Walker glance down to me. He eased his hold on me, releasing me from that convenient little spot tucked up against his hard body.

I jumped back, eying him. I wanted to tell him I didn't need his help, but I wasn't stupid. I knew the second I was lifted off the floor, I had no chance against the drunk man. I looked at Walker and took a breath, willing my pulse to slow the hell down and every cell in my body to stop it with the happy dance.

"Thank you. I should've kicked him in the balls first," I finally said.

Walker's lips quirked in a smile, immediately sending my belly into a series of flips. "That might've done the trick."

Megan jumped in. "Thank you so much. He was so drunk, and he just wouldn't leave me alone."

I glanced her way. "I don't know if you should be thanking me," I said wryly.

"Well, thank you both. I'm going to take that as my cue to call it a night." At that, she waved at us both and hurried through the crowd to sidle up to one of her friends.

That left me alone with Walker. I was acutely aware of my pulse, its thrumming beat careening through my body at a breakneck pace. "Well, um, thanks again I'm not sure where Joe went—"

Walker chuckled at that. "Oh, he's making out with some girl in the back."

"What? You have got to be fucking kidding me," I muttered.

"I'm definitely not kidding. You can see him," he said, nudging his chin toward the swinging half door that led behind the bar to the kitchen and storage.

Glancing over my shoulder, I saw Walker was quite right. Joe was deep into making out with a woman against the wall in the hallway. I was actually relieved to have something else to be annoyed about. I didn't know what to think about my body's haywire reaction to getting up close and personal to Walker, so any distraction was welcome.

"I have to get back to work, so thanks again," I said, giving him a last glance and a nod as I strolled past him. As if to remind me that while I might be trying to ignore it, my body knew what it wanted, my belly shimmied as I strode quickly past him and stepped behind the bar again.

WALKER

Jade Cole practically ran past me, and my eyes were a magnet on her, tracking every step. Her glossy dark hair fell like a river down her back, the long tresses catching the light and swinging as she moved. I couldn't help but think how it would feel to spin that glorious hair around my fist.

Only Jade—barely up to my chin and maybe a third the size of the drunk guy she'd taken on—would think it made sense to try to kick him out like that on her own. But then, Jade didn't strike me as the kind of girl to ever back down.

As I turned to walk away, it didn't slip my notice that the side of my body where I'd pulled her close felt like it was on fire. Jade was a petite bundle of curves with enough sass and spirit to tempt me beyond all reason.

With a mental shake, I walked away, telling myself to remember all the reasons why I'd avoided spending much time alone with Jade. I had once spent roughly fifteen minutes in the car alone with her when I gave her a ride home. That short span of time had made me question whether I'd previously understood what the concept of chemistry meant. Chemistry between two people, that is. I didn't quite know how it was possible, but the space in my car during that time felt as if lightning had struck, every particle in the air vibrating from its lingering power.

Riiiiight. I didn't need to wonder what Jade might be doing tonight after the bar closed, most definitely not.

I returned to the booth where I'd stopped to catch a few drinks with the guys on my first responder crew. Dawson, as usual, was cracking jokes. Jade's brother Lucas was nowhere to be found. Most likely because that man was about as head over heels in love as a man could be with his girlfriend, Valentina.

Slipping into the booth, I took a long

drag on my beer, glancing over when I heard my name. "What?"

"Well, look at that. He speaks," Dawson teased.

I rolled my eyes. "Of course. You've heard me speak plenty of times."

"Well, you were Jade's savior there. I was commenting that will further the legend," he said.

"Huh? What legend?" I asked cautiously as I glanced around the table.

Wade waggled his eyebrows. "Ever since you rescued that girl from the climbing accident a few weeks back, she's been spreading rumors about how hot you are and how you're the best rescuer." He added air quotes around the word best.

"What? I was just doing my job. All of y'all have rescued people. This is not just a me thing."

Jackson winked and shrugged. "She's just got the hots for you. It'll blow over. Plus, you're still considered new around here, so you're more exciting than the rest of us."

"What the hell? I've lived here for six months," I muttered.

Dawson chuckled. "Six months is nothing. People are just curious. Plus, you're single."

"That's how I like it. I plan to keep it that way," I replied.

"That's only going to make you enigmatic," Wade offered.

"A-plus for vocabulary," Dawson chimed in with a wink.

"Fuck enigmatic. There is no mystery about me. I mind my own business," I countered.

I did, in fact, mind my own business. I also had zero interest in romance. I'd been there, done that, and taken a blow. I was all fucking set with romance.

The night meandered along. I decided to cut out early, if only because I was legitimately tired. Between some training that morning on a climbing wall, and a hiking rescue that afternoon, I was ready to try to catch some shut eye.

Stepping out into the cool spring darkness, I paused to stare at the sky for a few beats. Clouds drifted in front of the half moon, stars glittering in between them. The mountain ridge ahead was silhouetted in the darkness with a silver shaft of moonlight angling across part of it.

Lowering my gaze, I began walking toward my truck. A scuffing sound drew my attention. I didn't see anyone as I glanced around the parking lot until my eyes landed on the dumpster in the far corner.

The moment my eyes landed on the silhouette of the bottom perched at the top of the dumpster, I knew I was staring at Jade Cole's luscious ass.

She was kicking her legs. I didn't know how, but she seemed stuck. My boots moved toward her. My greedy eyes took the moment to absorb the sight of her. *Cut the shit*, my good angel said. *She's not on display personally for you.*

"Jade?" I stopped beside the dumpster, puzzling about how she got herself half stuck in the dumpster.

"Walker?" she returned, her tone slightly surprised.

"Yep, that would be me. Need some help?"

"Does it look like I need help?" she countered swiftly, her annoyance clear.

I bit back a laugh. "I'm not quite sure because I'm guessing you would jump down. But you're not trying, so something's up."

Stepping closer, I peered over the edge of the dumpster to investigate. Nothing was immediately evident. "Uh, I'm not sure how I can help."

"I got caught," she muttered, reaching her hand toward her waist.

Tracking her motion, I noticed her belt loop had snagged on a hook sticking out inside the edge of the dumpster.

"Damn. Stop wiggling, Jade. That nail's rusty and you're gonna scratch yourself if you're not careful."

"Tell me something I don't know, genius," she retorted.

"How attached are you to that belt loop?" I asked as I leaned over to peer closer.

Jade turned her head to the side, somehow managing to be sexy as hell even though she was in a decidedly awkward position.

"Not at all. I already tried to tear it, but no luck."

Sliding my hand in my pocket, I pulled out the small pocket knife I kept on me at all times for no particular reason, except for the fact that it came in handy time and again. Flicking it open, I stepped closer to her hips. "I'm gonna cut it, okay?"

"Of course, cut away. And, of course you have a pocket knife. You're *that* kind of guy."

I chuckled as I pressed my hand against her hip, just enough to lift it slightly so I could get a better view of where her belt loop was hitched on the hook. In a second, I sliced clean through it. She started to wiggle down, beginning to come down sideways.

Dropping the knife to the ground, I caught her in the nick of time as she stumbled to the ground when one of her cowboy boots struck the pavement. "Easy," I murmured as I steadied her.

Jade straightened, lifting a hand and brushing a few locks of hair out of her eyes. She blew a puff of air to send the last errant lock off her forehead. Stepping back, she sighed. "Thank you. I guess I owe you twice now."

"You don't owe me. I did what anyone would do."

Jade's gaze was considering as she stared at me in the parking lot with moonlight gilding her hair in silver. "Actually, that's not true. That asshole got going in the bar and you were the only person who even noticed. Plus, not everyone carries a pocket knife everywhere," she said, her tone dry.

I felt my lips kick up on one side. "I suppose not. Maybe it's none of my business, but what the hell were you doing climbing into the dumpster anyway?"

Jade rolled her eyes. "When I threw the trash bag in, one of my bracelets flew off my wrist," she explained, gesturing to her now bare wrist.

I couldn't say I'd considered it much, but I was aware she usually wore a wide silver bracelet on her wrist. I shouldn't have known that detail, but then every detail about Jade appeared to be burned into my brain without any effort on my part.

"Well, then we should find it. Tell me what it looks like." Without thinking further, I curled a hand on the side of the dumpster and jumped in.

When I glanced back to Jade, for once, her usual guarded expression had subsided. Her eyes were wide open and her mouth had fallen open. "Tell me what it looks like," I repeated.

She snapped her mouth shut, a wondering laugh escaping. There I stood, in the fucking dumpster mind you, and the sound of her throaty laugh elicited a low pull in my gut. Much as I preferred not to want Jade, I did. As much as I needed air to breathe, my body wanted Jade. Which was why I generally avoided her.

"It's silver," she finally said. "About this wide." She held up her fingers to demonstrate.

Glancing down to where my boots were

planted amongst garbage bags, I scanned for a glimpse of silver. When the moon and the dim light in the far corner of the parking lot didn't do me any favors, I slipped my phone out of my pocket and tapped the flashlight button. Once the bright light came on, I moved it in a pattern over the trash bags, my eyes stopping when the light reflected off something.

I walked a few steps over and reached down into the not-so-pleasant smelling trash. "Got it," I called, holding the bracelet aloft.

When I straightened, Jade, who didn't smile very often, graced me with a beauty. Her lips curled at the corners and her eyes tilted. "Wow! You found it."

Stepping back to the edge of the dumpster, I handed it to her before resting one hand on the edge and hopping over to land on the pavement beside her. Jade spun the bracelet in a circle in her hands, still smiling. This time when her gaze met mine, it was almost shy. "That was really sweet, Walker."

Oh hell. Sweet was not an adjective I was usually labeled with. I felt an unbidden smile tugging up the corners of my mouth.

"Well, now I owe you three times. Don't argue the point," she said quickly when I opened my mouth to do exactly that.

I did the craziest thing next. "Actually, if you insist, I do have a favor I could use some help with."

"Anything."

"I have to go to a wedding, and I could use a date." I couldn't believe I'd actually said that, but the words were out, so there was no going back.

For the second time in my experience, Jade's mouth fell open. After an electrifying moment of silence, she asked, "A date?"

Maybe I hadn't thought too much about this, or not at all, but I wasn't one to back down. "Yep. A date."

She rested a hand on her hip. "Is this a joke?"

I shook my head slowly, a plan materializing in my brain. "Definitely not. Next weekend. A good friend of mine is getting married, and I'd rather not go solo." Just as I began to think that I didn't want to have to explain why to Jade, her question sliced through the pause.

"And why not? You're not exactly the kind of man who can't handle a wedding on his own."

I decided right then and there that I was going to dive into this insanity. I had an itch to scratch, a quite specific itch. She could be my date for the weekend, and we could burn this fire between us to ashes.

If I had to explain why, then so be it. "Look, it's one of my best buds. I was going to go without a date and say fuck it all, but my ex is going to be there."

"You have an ex?" Jade interjected, arching a brow so high, I was surprised it didn't fly off her forehead.

"Yes. I have an ex. We broke up because she screwed around on me with my best friend's brother. I'm not sure what's up, but she's been texting and calling lately. I get the idea she wants another chance. I'd rather her not get *any* ideas," I said flatly. I didn't feel much of anything about it and was more than glad to close the door on that whole mess. It was just I preferred not to have any pitying gazes cast my way during the wedding, and I definitely preferred my ex to consider me off limits. That was easier if she thought I was dating someone.

Several things flashed through Jade's eyes, ending with her eyes narrowing in anger. "Oh, that's *not* cool. I'm guessing the brother will be at the wedding."

I nodded. "Yeah. It's his family. I'm well over my ex, before you worry that that's what this is about. But, I'd prefer she leave me alone."

"I'm your girl," Jade said, nodding vigorously.

"Okay then. Sounds like we have a plan. Can you handle a long weekend out of town —three days?"

"I'll make sure I can. I'll be the best date you ever had, and I'll make her feel like the cheating bitch she is."

I couldn't help but laugh. "Tell me where to pick you up. It's next weekend."

"Here, let me give you my number," Jade said. "Just text me the details. I'll rearrange my schedule and you'll have me. By the way, I would've done this even if you hadn't saved my ass from that fool and then gotten me out of the dumpster and found my bracelet. It's just the principle, you know?"

"Oh, I do."

After I entered Jade's number in my phone, I watched as she strolled back into the bar. Her cowboy boots struck on the gravel with each step and her hair swung at her waist. Electricity sizzled up my spine. Three days with Jade was going to be interesting.

· · ·

———

Coming June 2020!
If We Dare

If you love hot, small town romance, take a visit to Willow Brook, Alaska in my Into The Fire Series. Check out Burn For Me - a second chance romance for the ages. It's FREE on all retailers! Don't miss Cade & Amelia's story!

Go here to sign up for information on new releases: http://jhcroixauthor.com/subscribe/

5) Follow me on Instagram at https://www.instagram.com/jhcroix/

6) Like my Facebook page at https://www.facebook.com/jhcroix

———

Swoon Series
    This Crazy Love
    Wait For Me
    Break My Fall
    Truly Madly Mine
    Still Go Crazy
    If We Dare - coming June 2020!
    Steal My Heart - coming August 2020!

Into The Fire Series
Burn For Me
Slow Burn
Burn So Bad
Hot Mess
Burn So Good
Sweet Fire
Play With Fire
Melt With You
Burn For You
Crash & Burn

Brit Boys Sports Romance
The Play
Big Win

Out Of Bounds
Play Me
Naughty Wish
Diamond Creek Alaska Novels
When Love Comes
Follow Love
Love Unbroken
Love Untamed
Tumble Into Love
Christmas Nights
Last Frontier Lodge Novels
Take Me Home
Love at Last
Just This Once
Falling Fast
Stay With Me
When We Fall
Hold Me Close
Crazy For You
Just Us
Catamount Lion Shifters
Protected Mate
Chosen Mate
Fated Mate
Destined Mate
A Catamount Christmas
The Lion Within
Lion Lost & Found

ACKNOWLEDGMENTS

To every reader who takes a chance on my stories. Thank you!

My editor made sure I gave Grace & Boone my best. Terri D. scours for all the details I miss.

Many thanks to the last round of readers who triple check for me - Janine, Beth P., Terri E., Heather H., & Carolyne B.

To my friends and family for being there in every way that matters. To my dogs for reminding me every single day what love is.

xoxo

J.H. Croix

ABOUT THE AUTHOR

USA Today Bestselling Author J. H. Croix lives in a small town in the historical farmlands of Maine with her husband and two spoiled dogs. Croix writes contemporary romance with sassy women and alpha men who aren't afraid to show some emotion. Her love for quirky small-towns and the characters that inhabit them shines through in her writing. Take a walk on the wild side of romance with her bestselling novels!

Places you can find me:
jhcroixauthor.com
jhcroix@jhcroix.com

 facebook.com/jhcroix

twitter.com/jhcroix

 instagram.com/jhcroix

www.ingramcontent.com/pod-product-compliance
Lightning Source LLC
Chambersburg PA
CBHW070757190726
48292CB00002B/560